Buried
Secrets

Books by Jane Tesh

The Grace Street Mysteries
Stolen Hearts
Mixed Signals
Now you See It
Just You Wait
Baby, Take a Bow
Death by Dragonfly
Gone Daddy Blues

The Madeline Maclin Mysteries
A Case of Imagination
A Hard Bargain
A Little Learning
A Bad Reputation
Evil Turns
A Wild Ride

Stand Alone Mysteries
Ghost Light

Buried Secrets

A Madeline Maclin Mystery

Jane Tesh

Savvy Press

First Edition 2020

Library of Congress Control Number: 2020935851

ISBN: 9781939113726   Trade Paperback
ISBN: 9781939113733   Kindle

Savvy Press
481 Beattie Hollow Rd
Salem NY 12865
www.savvypress.com
info@savvypress.com

Cover design: Fervor Creative

Printed in the United States of America

To my friend, Sylvia Chilton,
who loves Jerry
almost as much as I do.

Thanks once more to my editor, Ellen Larson,
my cover artist, Francois Thisdale,
and my proofreader, Linda Parks.

The fatal stone is closed above me—
Behold my tomb. The light of day
I shall see no more.

—From *Aida* by Giuseppe Verdi

CHAPTER ONE

The last person I expected to knock on the office door of Madeline Maclin Investigations that bright Monday morning in September was my ex-husband. But here he stood, looking uncomfortable, as if my small town of Celosia, North Carolina was a foreign country and he didn't know the language. Bill lived in Parkland, a much larger city, about thirty miles away. I hadn't seen him in months, and quite frankly, that was fine by me. He wore his usual khaki pants and navy blue golf shirt, a style I liked to call Preppy Casual. His dark hair was perfectly trimmed and his tan made his forced smile even whiter.

"Good morning, Bill," I said as pleasantly as possible. "What can I do for you?"

"Madeline. Good to see you."

Oh, was it? Take the high road, Madeline. "Thanks. Have a seat."

He sat down in the beige and green chair I have for clients. The window was closed, the air conditioner humming. He looked around. I'm not sure what he thought of the small room, but I loved the lush patterned walls I'd painted with flower designs, the bookshelf filled with items such as the stuffed toy frog my grand-mother had made, sea shells from my honeymoon in Bermuda, and a few of my smaller pen and ink sketches, including my favorite portrait of Jerry on our front porch, his eyes alight and his grin hinting at mischief.

Bill shifted in the chair. "I've seen your little show on YouTube. What's it called? *Crown to Crime*? Something like that. You're not recording anything right now, are you?"

Madeline Maclin: From Crown to Crime was a program on my YouTube channel about the life and adventures of an ex-beauty queen slash detective in a small North Carolina town. Which is what I am. "Not today," I replied.

Bill relaxed slightly. "How've you been, Madeline? Does Celosia have enough business for your agency?"

More than I ever would have imagined, although at the moment, my cases were down to Juniper Crinshaw's missing necklace and a potted plant another client was certain had been stolen off her front porch. "I'm doing well, thank you. What's this all about, Bill? Do you have a crime for me to solve?" I had a sudden stab of conscience. "Tina's all right, isn't she? And the kids?" Bill had always wanted children, something I couldn't handle at the time. At last count, he and second wife Tina had three, all girls, all saddled with unusual names: Halston, Foster, and Darlan Kyle. I was pretty sure that had been Bill's idea.

"They're fine. I've come here because—well, this is a sensitive matter, and I'd rather not have it all over Parkland. I've gotten myself into a situation."

I waited. I'd been attracted to Bill's dark good looks, his ambition, and his positive energy. Our marriage went well at first—until I realized that his ambition and energy were spent on his never-ending need for power and glory. And conquest.

"What's her name?"

He gave me a sheepish sideways look, a look that used to charm me until I realized his bad boy act wasn't an act. "Nadia Conrad."

Again, I waited.

"You see, Tina had a lot of trouble with the last baby, and we hired Nadia about a year ago to look after the other kids until Tina could manage things and—"

I couldn't believe it. "The nanny? My God, Bill, of all the relationship clichés."

He held up a hand. "Now hang on. I thought I was doing the right thing giving this woman a job. She was great with the children, and Tina liked her. I just—well, I couldn't help myself."

"And I can't help you," I said. "You need a lawyer."

"Let me finish. Everything was going great, the household was running smoothly, Tina was happy, Nadia was happy."

"Tina didn't know, did she?"

"No, of course not," he said, as if I'd said something improper. "Why upset her? I was planning to end it last Tuesday, but Nadia didn't show up for work. I called her number and there was no answer. I called the service she worked through, and they said she'd asked for time off, which was news to me. I figured she wanted to end our arrangement, too, and didn't know how to tell me. But since then, I haven't heard a word from her. I'm afraid something's happened to her. That's why I came to you."

No, you're afraid she'll tell Tina about the affair. "If you think she's missing, that would be a case for the Parkland police. Have you notified them?" I'd pushed my luck with the Parkland PD during my last case, which had involved my mother and the Parkland art community. I didn't want to make a habit of invading their territory.

"There's no need to involve the police," Bill said. "Nadia grew up in Celosia. I thought you might know her, or know people who do."

Before I had time to process this information, Jerry came in carrying my breakfast, the famous bacon biscuits he made every morning down at Deely's Burger World. When he saw Bill, he stopped in his tracks.

The two men couldn't be more different, Bill, tall and rangy with dark brown hair and a superior air, Jerry, shorter and lighter, with light brown hair and gray eyes. But the difference went deeper than appearance. Bill was a throwback to the Fifties alpha male who believed women should keep house and look after the children. Jerry was a free spirit whose shady past made our life together a constant source of surprise.

Bill stood but didn't offer his hand. "Jerry."

"Bill."

"How are things in the underworld?"

"How's life in the Playboy mansion?"

Enough of this. "Guys."

Jerry set the paper bag with the biscuits on my desk. "Talk to you later," he said, and was gone.

I turned back to Bill. "Just because she's from Celosia doesn't mean this isn't a case for Parkland PD."

"I'm pretty sure she's here. The last time we talked, she said she was planning to visit Celosia soon to see some friends and her grandfather. She sent money to him, the money I paid her. So, I was supporting him, too. That has to count for something."

Only in your mind, Bill. "When did you last see her?"

"I saw her last Sunday, but we talked on the phone this past Monday, but, as I said, she didn't come into work on Tuesday and hasn't answered any of my texts. I thought she was going to Celosia Monday and coming back to Parkland that same day."

I made a note of this. "I'll look into it. What's the name of the service?"

"Home Helpers. Here's their number." He handed me his phone.

"And Nadia's number? And her address?"

"That's in there, too." He sat back as if he'd done me a favor. "That's great, Madeline, thanks. I know you'll be discreet."

Nadia lived at 1216 B Missouri Street. I copied the information into my phone and handed his back. "But you have to tell Tina."

"Hell, no."

"You can't have a healthy relationship and keep secrets like this."

"So you and Jerry tell each other everything?"

Jerry had kept his con life secret for a long time, but I liked to think I knew all about it now. Bill's question reminded me that Big Mike, the boss of the shady organization Jerry had left behind, was looking to have a talk with Jerry. For a while, it appeared that Jerry was next in line to run Big Mike's organization. Could Jerry say "no" if Big Mike popped the question now? I was certain he would. I hoped he would. Either way, this was not something I'd ever discuss with Bill. "Yes."

"Well, I'm not going to tell Tina."

"Then I'm not sure I can take your case."

He glowered a few moments, the same glower that had signaled the end of our relationship, an expression dangerously close to a pout. "I don't see why I should upset her."

"Wouldn't it be more upsetting if, God forbid, something has happened to Nadia, and the police decide you're a suspect?"

He wasn't convinced. "Then it's your job to find her before anything like that happens."

I'd forgotten how frustrating it was to argue with him. "I don't think I owe you anything, Bill."

"Please, Madeline, for old time's sake? I'll think about telling Tina, honest. My main concern is to find Nadia and make sure she's okay."

I'd also forgotten how quickly he could turn on the charm. But I lived with Jerry, so I knew real charm when I saw it, and this was a poor imitation. However, if Nadia was in Celosia, and I could help find her, I felt compelled to try.

"All right. Do you have a picture?"

Of course he did. He found it on his phone and showed it to me. The picture was of an exotic-looking young woman with dark hair worn long with bangs.

"What else can you tell me about her?"

Other than her age—twenty-five—and physical attributes, her way with the children, and her ties to Celosia, Bill knew very little.

"How did she feel about you cheating on Tina?" I asked. "You said the two women liked each other."

"It didn't seem to bother her, at all. I think she got a thrill out of it."

The World According to Bill. "She never threatened to black-mail you?"

"Of course not! We were consenting adults. People have af-fairs all the time, Madeline."

"Yes, I know." I treated him to a pointed stare.

He didn't apologize or seem the slightest bit embarrassed. He took out his wallet. "Look, whatever your fee is, I'll double it. I need Nadia found as quickly and quietly as possible. I think you'll agree it's in both our best interests this not be featured on your YouTube show as the Mystery of the Week."

He paid me, texted me the picture of Nadia, and left.

I would have no problem seeing his sordid affair exposed on YouTube or anywhere else, but it would break Tina's heart. I sat for a while, wondering if I'd done the right thing. Maybe Nadia didn't want to be found. It sounded as if she'd decided it was wrong to carry on with Tina's husband and then look after her kids as if nothing had happened.

I called Nadia's number and was directed to her voicemail. At the beep, I said, "Hello, Nadia. My name is Madeline Maclin, Home Helpers recommended you as someone who is very good with children. I'd like to talk to you about looking after my little ones. Please give me a call."

I gave her my contact information, thanked her, and ended the call. I unwrapped one of the bacon biscuits and enjoyed a couple of bites. Well, of course, Bill had made Nadia's "disappearance" all about himself. She needed time off, all right. Time off from Bill.

I finished the first biscuit, took a big drink of my coffee, and called Nell Brenner, police chief Gus Brenner's daughter. Nell was our local handywoman and my source of all things Celosian.

"Don't know much about Nadia," Nell said. I imagined her, tall and sturdy in her white painter's overalls, her blond ponytail sticking out the back of her baseball cap. "She was right younger than me, so we weren't in school together."

"Did you happen to see her when she was in town last week? I understand she came to Celosia to visit friends. I'm guessing these might have been school friends."

"No, I didn't see her. But you can check with Adelaide Felton. They used to hang out together. I think Adelaide's still in town."

"How about Nadia's grandfather?" I asked.

"He still lives on the farm up on Henderson Road."

I was about to thank her and end the call when she said, "I heard you're hunting for Juniper Crinshaw's necklace."

News flew around Celosia. "Yes, have you seen it?"

"No, and I don't want to. Don't suppose she told you about it being an alien artifact, did she?"

"She did not say anything about aliens."

"Well, I'd leave it alone if I were you."

"Nell," I said, "I seriously doubt there are aliens involved."

"You can't be too careful, Madeline. People have seen UFOs around here before."

"Recently?"

"No, but my dad's grandfather said years ago a farmer and his grandson were out raking in their hay when they saw this metallic cube hovering above the ground and spinning like a top. They say it slowly moved up, leaving a glowing ring and a patch of hay all twisted counter clockwise."

"I'm guessing no one got a picture of the cube," I said.

"Nope. But there's an alien hunter coming to town this week to research it. Rodman Fogarty. He wouldn't be coming if there wasn't something to it, would he?"

That explained Nell's sudden interest in the supernatural.

"And that part of the field never did grow anything again," continued Nell. "The farmer's passed away, but you know his grandson, R.W. Jessup."

R.W. Jessup was one of the older gentlemen who always sat in the same corner booth at Deely's, holding forth on political issues and things they didn't like in town. Jerry had nicknamed them The Geezer Club.

I didn't figure Nell for an alien enthusiast, but somehow it didn't really surprise me. "What exactly does this have to do with Juniper's necklace?"

"Didn't she tell you? She says it brings bad luck. It's probably got some kind of alien curse on it."

Not only alien but cursed. Jerry would love this.

"The necklace has its ways," Nell said, and she sounded so serious, I held back a laugh until after I'd thanked her for the information and ended the call.

I took out the photograph Juniper Crinshaw had given me. It was a picture of a silver necklace with nine jade green stones. The necklace looked as if it had been made in the 1920s. It did not look alien. All I could think of was, bring it on. What was one more crazy thing this morning? Philanderin' Bill and the Missing Nanny. Honestly.

I found a number for Adelaide Felton in one of the older Celosia phone books I kept in my office. A message informed me that the number was no longer in service. So, a dead end there. Time for Biscuit Number Two.

"Is he gone?"

I looked up. Jerry stood in the doorway. "All clear," I said.

He came in and perched on the edge of my desk. "What in the world did he want?"

I turned the biscuit, looking for the right spot for maximum crunch. "He asked me to help find the children's nanny. Naturally, he was having an affair with her."

"Naturally."

After a satisfying mouthful, I reached for another napkin.

"Now she's disappeared, and he's afraid something's happened to her, but her employer says she asked for time off. I think the nanny, Nadia Conrad, got wise to Bill's tricks and decided to break off whatever they had going."

"Why did he come to you?" Jerry asked. "Doesn't he live in Parkland?"

"Looks like Nadia was headed here when last heard from. She's from Celosia."

"Did Bill hire you? Did he actually pay you?"

I showed him Bill's check. "Yes, he did."

Jerry took the check and turned it over as if expecting it to be counterfeit. "It's odd he should show up after all this time."

Jerry was used to looking for angles, but I didn't think Bill wanted anything except to keep Tina in the dark.

He handed the check back. "Will this be another exciting episode of *From Crown to Crime?*"

"Oh, no," I said. "As much as I'd like the world to know what a cad Bill is, Tina doesn't deserve to be humiliated for a YouTube show."

I glanced at my watch. Was it only nine-thirty? I felt as if my conversation with Bill had taken forever. "I don't have to be at Juniper's until three-thirty. Let's go talk to Nadia's grandfather and see what we can find out."

CHAPTER TWO

The Conrad farm on Henderson Road was a sprawling disorganized piece of land five miles from town, consisting of an unkempt pasture, a weathered barn leaning against a set of tumbledown pig pens, and a farm house that even with a generous amount of imagination had never looked good in a previous life.

I parked my light blue Mazda in the dirt driveway next to barrels overflowing with trash, a rusty tractor, and what looked like the world's oldest pickup truck. An ancient hound dog lying on the porch lifted its head and gave a token woof.

Jerry unbuckled his seat belt and got out. "Ten bucks says Mr. Conrad will be carrying a shotgun and demand we get off his property."

A wizened elderly man in faded jeans, a cap, and a long sleeved shirt came out of the house. He was carrying a shotgun, but all he said was, "Ain't lost, are you?"

"No," I said. "We live in the old Eberlin place. I'm Madeline Maclin and this is Jerry Fairweather. I run a home business, and Jerry works at Deely's."

He set the shotgun aside and squinted at me. "Didn't think

we'd met. I don't get to town often." He shook hands with me and with Jerry. "Albert Conrad. What can I do for you folks?"

"Is Nadia here?" I asked. "We'd like to talk to her."

"She ain't here right now." Another squint. "What would you want to talk to her about?"

"We're interested in talking to her about looking after my niece," I said. "Are you expecting her any time soon?"

"She was in town for a few days last week. Came by on Monday and stayed the night. Then she was going to visit friends a couple of days. Probably back in Parkland by now. The folks at Home Helpers didn't give you her number? Hang on, I got it here somewhere." He dug in the pocket of his overalls for a worn wallet. He opened the wallet and took out a creased piece of paper. "That's it."

Even though Bill had given me Nadia's number, I thanked Mr. Conrad and copied the number into my phone. "She sounds like the perfect person for our family."

"Yeah, she's a right sweet girl," he said. "She's always talking about them little girls she looks after. Give her a call and see."

Jerry wandered off to look around. The hound dog watched him, but made no effort to defend its territory. Mr. Conrad didn't seem to mind.

"Has Nadia always wanted to work with children?" I asked.

He squinted again in thought. "Can't say as I recall. Only thing she wanted to do was get out of Celosia. Can't say I blame her. Really nothing for her here. She worked at the grocery store till she saved up enough money to move to Parkland. Said she didn't want to move too far away."

"How does she like living in Parkland?"

He took off his cap to scratch his thin hair and replaced it firmly. "It was rough at first, but she stuck it out. She's a hard worker."

"I know what it's like to start over in a new town," I said. "It's taken me almost two years for my business to catch on."

"Well, she left Celosia a year ago. It took a while to get used to Parkland, but she really likes it now," he said.

"I imagine she has lots of friends there."

"Yeah, she's mentioned one woman in particular, someone who was right nice to her, showing her around, that sort of thing."

"Did she mention this woman's name?"

"Gabrielle something. Last name's Gray, I think. Could be Graham."

"Lots of friends here in Celosia, too?"

"Yeah, some school friends. Didn't none of them ever come up to the farm."

No doubt Nadia didn't want her friends to see where she lived. "Well, I'm sure she was lucky to have you."

"Yeah, Nadia's folks ran off some time ago and left her with me." He looked out across the yard as if seeing that day. The hound dog raised its head and gave him a worried look. He patted the dog's head. "Don't know where they are and don't care. They was lousy parents. My son never did have good sense, and the woman he married was some foreign girl. Maybe they ran back to wherever she was from."

"It sounds like you've done a good job raising Nadia, Mr. Conrad," I said.

He nodded and gave the dog another pat. "I like to think so."

I wrote down my phone number and handed it to him. "Thank you for Nadia's number. If you hear from her, please ask her to call me."

"Sure will."

Jerry had circled back to the car, and we got in. I told him what I'd learned from Nadia's grandfather. "It's not much to go on," I said. "What about you?"

"I was hoping to find a still. I guess we have to be further up in the hills for that." He hooked his seat belt. "You owe me at least five bucks for the shotgun."

I put the car in gear and drove back down the dirt driveway to Henderson Road. I pulled into the parking lot of the Henderson Baptist Church and tried Nadia's number again. All I got was the same message saying Nadia Conrad wasn't available, please leave your number and a brief message.

"She's off the grid," I said.

"Putting as much distance as she can between herself and Bill."

"Nell gave me the name of one of Nadia's friends, but her phone number's no longer in service," I said. "Why don't we ride over to Parkland and see if Nadia's gone back home?"

***

Someone had decided to name all the streets in Nadia's housing development after states, so after turning down Wisconsin Avenue and making a left onto Delaware Lane, we came to the Deluxe Apartments at 1216 Missouri Street. I would've named them the Average Apartments. They were plain brick with white shutters and sad-looking boxwoods leaning under the windows.

To Jerry's disappointment, apartment B was on the first floor. He always enjoyed a bit of second story work.

We didn't see a car in the space marked for apartment B. I rang the doorbell. After a long wait, I peeked in the window but could see only a small plaid sofa and a little round table with a lamp on it.

"Nobody home," I said.

No one answered at apartment A or C, but we met a man out by the mailboxes who said he knew who Nadia was but couldn't recall the last time he'd seen her.

Back in my car, I looked up Gabrielle Gray. "Here's a possibility," I said. "There's a realtor in town named Gabrielle Gray." When I tried the number, a pleasant woman's voice answered. I told her I was looking for Nadia Conrad, and I had gotten her name from Nadia's grandfather.

"You must come over right away," she said. "I'm located in the Oasis Lofts downtown."

***

The Oasis Lofts were classy enough to have an intercom. One of the little gold buttons had the initials "G.G." on the label. I pressed the button, and when a woman's voice answered, I said, "This is Madeline Maclin."

"Come on up. I'm on the penthouse floor."

The front door clicked and Jerry pushed it open. We made our way to the elevators through an elegant lobby decorated with gold tiles and potted palm trees. Once we'd reached the top floor of the Oasis Lofts, the elevator opened onto a vast living space surrounded by windows that gave a spectacular view of the city. Gabrielle Gray was a tall beautiful woman in her thirties with dark brown skin and honey-gold hair pulled up into a style that made her look as if she were wearing a crown. She wore a flowing silk caftan patterned in green and blue, large dangling gold hoop ear-rings, and several gold necklaces. She extended a gold tipped hand.

"Ms. Maclin, I'm so worried about Nadia. This isn't like her, at all. I've tried to reach her, and either her phone is dead, or she's not answering any calls. Please, come in, sit down."

"Thank you," I said. "This is my husband, Jerry Fairweather."

"Delighted to meet you."

"Actually, Ms. Gray, I'm a private investigator, and I'm looking for Nadia."

"Well, thank goodness someone is taking this seriously," she said. "Please, both of you have a seat. Would you care for a drink?"

We declined the offer of drinks. I sat down on a low white sofa. Gabrielle arranged herself in a white chair opposite. The glass coffee table and end tables had crystal pedestals that matched the crystals dangling from the chandelier. Everything in the room sparkled and gleamed and shouted wealth.

Jerry wandered to the nearest set of windows. "This is an amazing apartment, Ms. Gray. Mind if I look around?"

He used his best smile, and Gabrielle beamed back at him. "Go right ahead. And it's Gabrielle, please. You can see the whole city from here, and all the way to the Blue Ridge from the balcony."

"I'll bet the sunrises are spectacular."

"The sunsets are even better," she said with a coy fluttering of her eyelashes.

Jerry gave her another smile and strolled off to the kitchen.

"How did you meet Nadia?" I asked.

Gabrielle turned her gaze back to me. "By merest chance. She happened to come into the Red Ribbon Club one night during one of our fund-raising parties about a year ago. I was there with a cou-ple of my friends, and Nadia was so darling. Such an innocent. She said she came in because her favorite color was red. She had no idea it was a gay bar and all proceeds from sales went to AIDS research. I had to explain everything to her, and I mean everything. Of course, she was from Celosia, so that explained everything to me. After that I took her under my wing."

"Any particular reason why?"

She put one graceful hand to her heart. "I like to help people whenever I can. I found her a nice place to live at Deluxe Apartments. It's a nice neighborhood, although maybe a little shabby, but a place she could afford. She also needed a job, so I got her in touch with Home Helpers."

"Do you know anything about Bill Rosser?" I asked.

"Bill and I are old friends. It was just chance that Nadia's first job through Home Helpers was looking after his children. It really is the perfect fit. She fell in love with his children."

Old friends, indeed. "And with Bill, too?" I asked.

She gave me a respectful stare. "Well, I see you really are a detective. Bill's rich and handsome."

"And married."

Her expression changed. "If you're looking for dirt on Nadia, you're not going to get it from me."

"I'm not," I assured her. "I just want to find her. It seems she would have confided in you, that's all."

Once again she put her hand to her heart. "Not at first. And I didn't pry. But I know Bill. And Nadia—."

"As you said, she is not sophisticated."

"More than that. She is the sort of person other people would take advantage of. I encouraged her to stand up for herself. When she finally told me it was over, she said it was because she was through with keeping secrets and being used. I was proud of her."

When Jerry returned, he handed me a brochure. The front cover showed Gabrielle in a classy gold suit and sparkly blouse with the words "Gabrielle Gray, Realtor" printed in gold letters above her picture.

"You seem to be a very successful realtor, Gabrielle," he said. "There are some beautiful homes listed in there."

"Thank you," she said.

"A few more questions, if you don't mind," I said. "When was the last time you saw Nadia?"

She fingered one of her long earrings. "I'm trying to think. Last Tuesday? No, it was Monday. She stopped by to tell me she was going home to see her grandfather and would miss my weekend party and for me to say hello to everyone for her."

"Do you remember her mood?" I asked. "Was she looking forward to going home, or was this just something she had to do?"

"Oh, she was looking forward to it. I assumed she had broken it off with Bill, and was looking forward to seeing her old friends."

"Did she mention anyone by name? Adelaide?"

"No, but there was Coreen and Lon and Kathy, maybe?"

"Thank you," I said. "I appreciate the help."

"Tell me when you find her?" asked Gabrielle. "I'm so worried."

"I will," I said, and we left.

CHAPTER THREE

W ell, this gives me a good starting place," I said as we
drove home. "Hopefully, one of Nadia's friends
knows where she is."

"Home" was the Eberlin House, a large rambling farm house
that sat in the middle of a meadow filled with wildflowers. The
house had been left to Jerry by his eccentric Uncle Val and had
slowly evolved from ramshackle farm house and bat sanctuary to
a comfortable country home. I hadn't been thrilled by the place at
first. It was rundown, thick with dust, and way too much of a DIY
for Jerry and me to handle, but thanks to the help of Nell Brenner
we now had a house we could call our home.

We drove up the winding driveway and parked under one of
the large oak trees. Austin and Denisha waved from our front
porch. Austin, an energetic white boy, and Denisha, a self-assured
black girl, were close friends and might as well have been our children considering the amount of time they spent at our house and
the amount of our food they consumed. Since it was almost noon,
I wasn't surprised to see them.

Austin held up a cardboard box. "Come see our skinks!"

They'd each captured a skink for the Skink Race, a major event in Celosia's annual SkinkFest, which started this coming Friday. Jerry and I had been out of town the week of last year's SkinkFest, so we missed all the excitement. It was a big deal. Main Street would be closed off for the weekend so people could set up booths to sell food and crafts, and there would be games, contests, and live music, mostly bluegrass. When I asked why this festival was called SkinkFest, the locals explained that every other animal, fruit, vegetable, mineral, and famous battle had already been chosen by other towns. So twenty-five years ago, someone had suggested the small striped lizard with the detachable blue tail and lo, SkinkFest was born.

Jerry and I admired the fat black and white striped lizards with shiny blue tails. They scrabbled around in the box, looking for an escape.

"Mine's The Skinkinator," Austin said. "He's the biggest one, see?"

"That doesn't mean he's the fastest." Denisha said. "Jet Tail is going to leave all the other skinks in the dust. Oh, and Madeline, my aunt says we can share her church's booth on Main Street for SkinkFest. They're having a bake sale, but we can use one of the tables. You know, for my poetry books and our detective agencies. It'll be good publicity."

Denisha had decided to start her own detective agency. Her first case had been *The Mystery of the Missing Charm Bracelet*. She'd also written a book of poems, and our friend and local poet, Hayden Amry, had helped her put the book together and even organized a book signing for her at Georgia's Books, our local independent book store located on Main Street not too far from my office. She planned to sell her books during the SkinkFest street festival and had insisted I join her.

"Oh, yes," I said. "Good news."

"When we talked about it before, you said it would cost too much money to rent a booth on Main Street. Well, this solves our problem."

"Yes, it does," I said. "Thanks for taking care of that."

She turned to Jerry. "Jerry, are you going to write a song for the SkinkFest?"

"You mean it doesn't have one?" he said. "I would've thought such a momentous event had its own anthem. 'Skinks Forever,' or 'God Save the Skink.'"

"I'm only interested in the race," Austin said. "The Skinkinator is going to blow the tails off all competitors."

"You wish," Denisha said. "Jet Tail is much faster than your fat old lizard."

Before their argument came to blows, I invited them into the kitchen for lunch. They cheerfully made their own peanut butter and jelly sandwiches, and Jerry brought out the plastic container he always kept full of cookies. The kids settled at the white wooden table and between mouthfuls of cookie and gulps of cola, told us all the wonderful things available at the festival.

Ordinarily, the idea of skink races, a skink parade, and a skink ball would have Jerry making plans to take part, but although he made encouraging remarks to the kids, his gaze kept straying to the wide kitchen windows and the pleasant scene of the field behind our house. I wondered what he was thinking about and hoped it wasn't another unsettling development in Con World. I recalled Bill's snide remark: *So you and Jerry tell each other everything?*

For the longest time, I didn't know about Jerry's other life. In college, he was chasing fluffy little blonds, and I was good old dependable Mac. He had an easy way of making friends, which I envied, being brought up to be suspicious of all the other little pageant girls. I was so serious about my love of painting, so determined to be Something Else. I didn't really care what, as long as it didn't involve a runway and a tiara. Jerry brought me into his circle of fun-loving pals. It wasn't until much later I found out these pals played by their own set of rules.

Big Mike recruited Jerry into Con World while Jerry was still in college. The way I looked at it, Big Mike was not only Jerry's teacher but a father figure—and possibly my step-father figure if he continued his romantic pursuit of my mother, something I still couldn't get my mind around. Right now, the two of them were vacationing in Paris. I'd warned Mom that Big Mike's business dealings could be questionable, but she didn't seem concerned.

I used to dread hearing from my mother. Until I helped her clear her name during a murder investigation, she had nothing good to say about my chosen career path and always bemoaned the fact I'd never become Miss America. But since she'd met Big Mike, she'd become a different person. I was very glad my mother had found someone who made her happy, but I hoped he would soon tell her the truth.

Austin took a handful of cookies. "Jerry, did you know there's a man in town who says that aliens landed around here?"

"No, but that sounds reasonable."

"He's got this poster up at the theater. He's going to give a talk about it tonight and during the festival." He dug his cell phone from his jeans pocket. "The poster's really neat. I took a picture. Doesn't that sound cool, though? Maybe there's still some pieces of their spaceship lying around. Hey, Denisha, you want to go look for some?"

"No," she said. "I've got to get my books ready. Hayden's

meeting me at the copy shop later today to make sure they turn out the way I want them."

He groaned. "Those books of yours are ruining my life."

"Austin Terrell, you are being overdramatic."

Austin turned his phone so Jerry could see the picture of the poster. "You'll come help me look, won't you?"

Jerry's attention was caught, but instead of his usual interested expression, his brow furrowed. He handed me the phone so I could read the brightly colored poster. "Aliens Landed in Celosia!" it announced in black and gold letters. "Professor Rodman Fogarty invites you to experience the unveiling of the unknown as he reads from his latest best-seller, *True Invasion*, tonight at the Celosia Little Theater at 8. Was the Carson Crater the site of a UFO landing? Did aliens make a home in Carson's Cave? Are there traces of alien DNA in the very soil of Celosia? Come discover the facts of this amazing incident!"

The second mention of Fogarty that day. Maybe the aliens had come back for their necklace. I gave Austin his phone. "Sounds impressive."

"I know where that Carson's Crater is, and the cave. Let's go."

"Tell you what," Jerry said. "I have to make a couple of phone calls, and then I'll go with you. Don't go into any sort of cave by yourself."

"I've been in the cave. It's not really all that big."

"You shouldn't go in that cave," Denisha said. "My aunt said somebody died in there."

Austin immediately took offense. "They did not! She's just trying to scare you. Anyway, I'm heading for the crater first."

"The crater's not dangerous," Denisha said. "It's just a big shallow hole. We've been in it dozens of times."

Austin bristled at this criticism of the crater as a shallow hole. "Yeah, but we never knew it was made by a flying saucer."

"No, it wasn't."

"How do you know?"

Jerry forestalled any further argument. "I'd like to see the crater and the cave, so why don't you check out the crater and come back? I should be ready by then."

Austin agreed, and after the kids finished eating, he hopped on his bright red four-wheeler and roared off in the direction of Carson's Crater. Denisha got on her bike and rode off along the trail they'd made through the neighboring field, heading for home and her poetry books.

I asked Jerry about his reaction to the poster.

"I know Professor Rodman Fogarty," he said.

"Oh, good lord," I said in mock exasperation. "How many people were in Con School with you? Just when I think we're done, another one pops up."

"No worries. This guy was before my time. He's been out of the game for over five years. He had some sort of mind altering experience and went way overboard on the alien thing, UFO conspiracies, crop circles, you name it. This must be his latest obsession."

"So, a harmless fanatic, we hope?"

"Fogarty usually keeps to the big cities. It's odd he decided to come to Celosia. If there's a connection here, I need to know it. But not now. I need to call Tucker and see if his special new rose has bloomed yet."

Jerry's younger brother, who still lived at the Fairweather mansion, was an avid gardener specializing in roses. His gardens were spectacular. The last time we'd visited, he'd told us of his plans for his own hybrid rose, a white rose with touches of gold he'd named "Lillian," in honor of their mother.

"Ask him to send pictures," I said.

"If he'll let me," Jerry said. "Sometimes these new roses are kept secret until they're premiered at some big flower show."

"Well, then, please tell him congratulations."

***

While Jerry made his phone calls, I received a phone call of my own.

It was Eloise Michaels, a member of the Women's Improvement Society.

"Madeline, I hope you're not too busy," she said. "The Women's Improvement Society is taking part in SkinkFest this year, and we thought a pageant would be just the thing. I know it's last minute. What do you think? Would you be willing to advise our pageant committee? This won't be a serious competition, of course."

I might as well accept the fact that my life would never be pageant-free. Only a month ago, I'd been a consultant and judge for the Miss Streetwise Pageant, although this had been a return favor for another of Jerry's acquaintances' help on a case. "Would this be Miss SkinkFest?"

"Oh, yes. I think it would be a lot of fun, don't you?"

Fun, perhaps. Drama, definitely. You can't have a group of women competing for a beauty title—even a comic one—and not lose some sequins.

"Could you meet me at Deely's this afternoon around two? The committee has everything organized, but I'd love to have your input."

"Sure," I said. My meeting with Juniper Crinshaw wasn't until three-thirty, and Heritage Lane, where she lived, was only a ten minute drive. Plenty of time to call Nadia's friends.

***

An internet search found Nadia's senior class and the last names of the friends Gabrielle had mentioned: Coreen, Lon, Kathy, and Patrick. The first one I reached was Kathy Holly.

She was a chatty Kathy. Her voice was pleasant and friendly, and I imaged she was the kind of person who—unlike me—kept up with everyone she'd ever gone to school with.

"I understand you know Nadia Conrad," I said.

"Oh, yes, we were good friends in high school," Kathy Holly said.

"I'm looking for someone to watch my niece, and her name was suggested. Then someone told me you might be able to help me. I need a few references before I call her."

"She doesn't live here anymore. She's in Parkland. But she's great with kids. I would definitely recommend her. Maybe you could take your niece to Parkland, or have Nadia come to Celosia."

"Thanks," I said. "Is there anyone else who knew her who might give me a good reference? My niece is a bit high strung, so I have to be especially careful who I hire to look after her."

"You can try Coreen Overmeyer," she said. "She's head of the Celosia Garden Club. She went to high school with Nadia and me."

"Thank you," I said. "I suppose Nadia comes back to Celosia every now and then to visit her friends."

Kathy's cheery tone went flat. "I haven't seen or heard from her in ages."

Hmm. So Nadia comes to Celosia after telling Bill she was going to visit friends, but doesn't call or visit Kathy Holly. Did she visit Coreen Overmeyer or some other friend? If not, what was she doing all week?

***

I went back to my Mazda and found the Celosia Garden Club listed with other civic organizations in the copy of the town directory I keep in the car. When I called, a lofty female voice said, "This is Coreen Overmeyer, president of the Celosia Garden Club and creator of the Overmeyer Prestige rose. I am involved with very important business at the moment. Please leave a message."

We were up to president now. "Good afternoon," I said. "My name is Madeline Maclin, and I'm doing a special program about your senior class for my YouTube channel series, *From Crown to Crime*. I'd like to interview you at your convenience." I left my number and ended the call. Perhaps that would intrigue President Overmeyer.

***

I had a few minutes before it was time to meet Eloise at Deely's, so I stopped by

the Super Food. Nadia's grandfather had mentioned she worked at the grocery store, and in Celosia everyone referred to the Super Food as the Grocery Store. It was exactly like every other Super Food, a vast area of gleaming floors and packed shelves. The manager, a trim woman with blond streaks in her brown hair, took time from supervising a young man shelving cartons of toothpaste to answer my questions.

"Yes, Nadia worked here for about two years, right after she got out of high school. She was a good worker, very focused, but she didn't want to work here forever. We were all sorry to see her go, but we were glad she found a good job in Parkland."

"Does she ever stop by to say hello?" I asked.

"Actually, she was here last Tuesday to see everyone." She frowned. "Is there a reason you're asking about her?"

"I heard she was really good with children," I said, "and I thought she might be available to watch my niece next week."

"She works for a company called Helping Hands," the woman said. "I'd call and ask them."

I thanked her and checked my phone. Two o'clock. Just enough time to get to Deely's.

CHAPTER FOUR

D eely's Burger World, where Jerry spent his mornings cooking breakfast biscuits, was the prime meeting spot for anyone who wanted to get caught up on the latest news and gossip. A few folks drifted in, taking seats on the silver stools with red plastic cushions at the counter and in the wooden booths with matching red plastic seats. Their friendly chatter blended with the sizzling sounds of burgers frying on the grill. Deely's had started out as an ice cream parlor, and there were still traces of its history in the etched window glass, the ornate clock hanging on the back wall, and the ancient Coke machine in the corner that Deely and Jerry had hauled up from the basement in hopes of restoring.

Eloise waved me over to a booth. She was a small gray-haired woman whose little beady eyes and sharp little nose reminded me of a mouse. She wore a striped blouse and khaki slacks, which I understood to be the official SkinkFest uniform. The pageant committee had already drafted a set of rules and a schedule for Miss SkinkFest, and Eloise was pleased when I approved. It did look like a fun event, including a contest for Little Miss and Little Mister SkinkFest and Miss Teen SkinkFest. There was no talent portion, only fancy dress with a skink theme. There would be prizes and crowns for everyone.

I read over the rules and schedule. "Looks like you've thought of everything," I said. "No entry fee?"

"No," Eloise said. "We're asking everyone to bring contributions for the food bank instead."

"Great idea. What about judges?"

"The mayor has agreed to judge, as well as the president of the Downtown Association, and we were hoping you'd agree."

This would be an amusing entry for *Crown to Crime*. "I'd be glad to."

She thanked me and insisted on buying me lunch. Since I'd only had a few cookies and some iced tea with the kids, I gratefully accepted her offer. Once we had our burgers, fries, and drinks, I asked her if she knew Nadia Conrad.

Eloise tugged the paper off her straw. "A nice young woman. Her grandfather did a good job raising her. I hear she's got a good job in Parkland. Why are you asking? She's not in trouble, is she?"

"I don't think so," I said. "But her employer in Parkland is concerned about her. He hasn't heard from her since last Monday. Her grandfather said she came to visit him on Monday. When's the last time you saw her?"

Eloise thought for a moment. "My goodness, I don't think I've seen her since she used to work at the grocery store."

"She has a couple of friends in town. One named Lon? Do you know him?"

She chose another French fry from the container. "Lon Forest. He lives with his mother out on Heritage Lane."

"Well, that's convenient," I said. Then, in answer to Eloise's puzzled look, "I'm on my way to see Juniper Crinshaw," I explained. "I'm looking for her necklace."

To my surprise, Eloise laughed. "That old thing? She's always losing it. She says it runs away from her."

"So you know about its alien ancestry?"

"Lord, yes, she's been talking about that for years." She wiped her fingers on her napkin. "She says the stones are from a meteorite that fell here years ago. She's never actually explained how the stones got made into a necklace, though."

"So you don't believe her story?"

"It's more likely she found it in that museum of hers."

"Museum?" I asked.

"You've never been to her house?"

"No."

"I'll bet she's got one or more of everything that ever existed," Eloise said with another snort of laughter. "I'll bet she's got a plaque in the Hoarders Hall of Fame. I'll even bet you anything the necklace is lost in all that mess. Juniper's a bit over dramatic."

Mentioning dramatics reminded Eloise of *Flower of the South*, and she spent the rest of our lunch relating the success of Celosia's outdoor drama and the Society's plans to revive it next summer.

"I'm really glad everything worked out," I said and checked my watch. "Thanks so much for lunch, but I'd better go. Juniper's expecting me at three-thirty."

"Tell her hello," Eloise said with a grin. "And look out for aliens."

***

Heritage Lane was a street in one of the older more run down neighborhoods in Celosia. From the outside, Juniper Crinshaw's house looked like a typical two story white clapboard with gray shutters and a porch with a roof that leaned slightly to the left. The yard needed mowing, but the bushes were trimmed. Flower boxes at the lower windows held a variety of scraggly chrysanthemums, and an empty bird feeder dangled from a metal crook. A large white cat regarded me indifferently from its perch on the porch railing.

Juniper met me at the door. She was a large woman with long gray hair tied in a braid. She wore a bright yellow smock over her tee shirt and jeans. She wiped her hands on the smock.

"Just finishing up some muffins. They'll be done in a few minutes."

She opened the door wider to let me come in, and I entered an alternate universe.

I'd been in homes where the owners were hoarders. This wasn't like that. Eloise Michaels had been right to call Juniper's house a museum. Everywhere I looked, I was confronted with glass cases and cabinets filled with collections of—things. One case was full of watches and rings. Another case was filled with stuffed birds. The long cabinet that stretched all the way down the hall held artifacts and curios that looked African. Carved masks, ceremonial swords, kimonos, kites, and fans decorated the walls. Two huge bookshelves were crammed with salt and pepper shakers. The house smelled strongly of potpourri.

"This is all very interesting," I said.

Juniper led the way to the kitchen past a bookcase filled with snow globes. "I couldn't decide what I wanted to collect, so I ended up collecting everything. Watch out for the umbrella stand."

I sidestepped a tall ceramic vase filled with a jumble of walking sticks and narrowly avoided stubbing my toe on a huge glass jar of marbles. Safely in the kitchen, I sat down in a folding chair at a card table piled with boxes of postcards.

Juniper opened a cabinet to get a glass, and I saw shelves loaded with all kinds of mugs. "I hope you have news about my necklace."

"No, I'm sorry, I don't."

The timer dinged on her stove. I noticed she had a whole row of timers, one of each color. "Muffins are done." She took the pan out. "We'll let them cool a little. Now, about my necklace."

"Right," I said. "I've asked several people about it, and someone said you thought it was an alien necklace."

"Oh, I'm certain it is." She gestured toward another room. "I collect rocks, too, and about ten years ago, I was out by Carson's Crater when I found what had to be a meteorite. I knew it was from space. I probably should've taken it to a museum, but it wasn't very big, and I really liked the pieces of green inside. So I had the pieces made into a necklace. Then things started happening."

Uh, oh. The Alien Curse Nell warned me about. "What kind of things?"

She moved another box off another folding chair and sat down. "The first time I lost the necklace, we had the worst drought we'd ever had in Celosia. After I found it, we had rain for a week. The second time, one of the actors borrowed it for a show up at the theater, and she fell and broke her leg right before opening night. The third time, I lent it to the Garden Club for someone to wear in a charity fashion show. Half the members got sick and they had to cancel the event. That's when I decided the necklace better stay here."

"Are you sure it isn't here?"

"Trust me, I have searched and searched. I'm sure all this looks like clutter to you, but it's organized clutter. Postcards go here. Rocks go there. Jewelry is kept in the second bedroom. Someone must have stolen it. Someone must have heard about its power."

"But you told me no one had come to the house in weeks before you noticed it was gone," I said.

"Right. I don't get many visitors."

It would take a very determined burglar to hunt through the mess to find anything valuable. I asked if she had an alarm system.

"So you're thinking someone broke in?" she said. "No, I don't have an alarm, but how would a thief know what to take? Even I don't know everything that's in here." She leaned forward, and her elbow sent a stack of postcards tumbling to the floor. "Madeline, I just had a thought. I don't know if you've heard about Professor Fogarty and his book, *True Invasion*? It's the true story of a UFO landing in Celosia, the same UFO that made Carson's Crater out in their field, and that very crater is where I found the meteorite." She sat back as if she had explained everything.

I wasn't exactly sure what she expected me to say. "I've seen the poster."

"Don't you get it? The necklace is trying to find its way home! That's why I keep losing it and why it causes so much trouble. It's made out of rock from another world."

"Unless the aliens come back for it, it's stuck here," I said.

"It's entirely possible they will come back." She bent down to retrieve the postcards and stacked them on the table. "I'll bet Fogarty will know. Are you planning to go to his lecture at the theater tonight?"

"I think maybe I should." Maybe her necklace planned to attend. I promised Juniper I'd continue my search and headed home.

***

Jerry texted to let me know he'd been called to Deely's to help unload some supplies. He was on his way home, too.

By the time I got to the house, it was almost five. Austin was waiting under one of the oak trees.

"Jerry had to go to Deely's," he said.

"Yes, thanks. He sent me a text," I said. "He'll be here soon. The cave's not going anywhere, is it?"

"No, but I'm ready to go now."

"Weren't you just there?" I asked.

"I was at the crater," he said, as if I were particularly dense. "Jerry said to wait for him before I went into the cave."

"It won't be dark until eight," I reminded him.

"But we need time to explore."

I knew how to distract him. "How about some chips?"

"Yeah!"

I found a bag of potato chips and two colas. We took our snack to the front porch and sat down in the rocking chairs.

Austin spoke through a mouthful of chips. "Denisha's no fun anymore. All she wants to do is write those poetry books."

"She's still your friend," I said. "I know she'd appreciate it if you support her new hobby."

"Yeah, well, I do, but shouldn't she support what I want to do? Sometimes I just want her to ride bikes or play video games like she did before, and she's not interested."

"She's taking part in the skink race, isn't she?"

He dismissed this with a wave of his hand. "She doesn't really want to. She just happened to catch a really big skink, which she thinks is going to win, but she'd better be ready for ultimate defeat."

Austin didn't have long to sulk about Denisha. His mood brightened as Jerry's Jeep came up the drive. As soon as Jerry parked and got out, Austin said, "Let's go!"

"I need to talk to Mac for a minute," Jerry said.

"Okay," Austin said. "I'll get ready."

He ran over to rev up his four-wheeler. Jerry took out his phone. "Tucker says hello, by the way, and here's a picture of Lillian."

The rose was stunning, the white petals edged in gold just as Tucker had hoped it would be. "He must be so proud," I said.

"And there's something else I probably should mention."

Oh, I knew that look. "Does this have anything to do with Big Mike's Big Decision?"

Jerry slid his phone back into his pocket. "Big Mike has decided on his successor. It isn't me."

I felt a huge rush of relief. Although Jerry said he didn't want the job, I knew that somewhere down deep he wanted to repay Big Mike for everything he'd done for him. Having him choose between me and the man who was like his father was not something I wanted him to do.

"Has word gotten around Con World that you are not the heir to the throne?" I asked. "Does this mean you're no longer a target?"

"Well, here's where it gets complicated," he said. "Big Mike has decided on a successor, but he hasn't named him or her yet. He told me I was not the lucky winner. But he didn't say who was."

"So people could still come after you?" Not long ago, we'd had a scary run-in with a group of thugs who wanted to take over Big

Mike's organization.

"Possibly, but since Big Mike took care of those guys, I doubt anyone else will be foolish enough to try."

"Okay, where does this leave my mother?" I asked.

"Safely with Big Mike, as he promised," Jerry said. "She's one of the main reasons he's leaving the game. He wants to spend more time with her."

"And I'm very happy for her, but I'm still really concerned about what happens when she discovers his true profession."

"By then he'll be out of the game," Jerry assured me.

"But just because he's no longer involved in his organization doesn't mean his enemies are going to fade away."

"Whoever he chooses to take over will be able to take care of everything."

"Just as long as it's not you," I said.

"Well, I told him that Fogarty was in town, and he did ask me to keep an eye on him and make sure he doesn't cause trouble. Big Mike likes this little town, and since he and your mom are probably going to get married, he'd like to keep everyone in his new family safe."

All I heard was "married." "Wait a minute. Is that why they're in Paris?"

"Well, he said it was a secret, but I think you knew it was going to happen."

"Are you guys coming or not?" Austin called over the roar of the engine.

"We're coming," Jerry called back. Then he turned to me. "Are you okay with all this, Mac?"

Married. I had to take another moment to process this. Ever since Big Mike asked me to introduce him to my mother, I could tell they were perfect for each other. While it was true I'd never seen my mother so happy, I couldn't shake my concerns about her future with a notorious con man. But wasn't I married to a notorious con man? If it worked for me, it ought to work for Mom. "I think so," I said.

"Are you ready to discover the truth behind Celosia's alien invasion?"

This sounded like the kind of ridiculous adventure I needed right now, and any adventure with Jerry along for the ride was fine with me.

"Beam me up," I said.

***

I hopped into the Jeep and we followed Austin's four-wheeler across the pasture. After bumping down another dirt road, we turned towards a large field. In the middle of this field was a scooped out place that, with the right amount of imagination, could be considered a meteor crater.

Austin bounded off the four-wheeler. "Neat, huh?" He slid down the edge of the crater and stood at the center.

Jerry and I also slid down. There was still plenty of sunlight to see every detail of the large depression. Very little grass grew in the crater. It was mostly sandy soil and eroded places in the sides where red clay made deep folds of dirt. I checked to see if Juniper's necklace was crawling around, searching for its way home.

Austin made a complete circle of the crater floor. "Denisha and I have been here lots of times, but I never thought about it being caused by space ships or saucers or anything like that. You reckon this Professor Fogarty knows what to look for?"

Suckers, mostly, I thought.

"We'll go to the lecture and find out," Jerry said. "I have to admit it doesn't look like much right now."

"Yeah, but it's still neat."

We admired the crater a few more minutes, and Jerry videoed me standing in it for *Crown to Crime.*

"Want to see the cave?" Austin asked. "It's not very far. We can walk."

We followed Austin across the field to a wooded area. Carson's Cave was set back in the trees, its opening marked by large rocks crowded around a gap in the hillside.

"It doesn't look like much," Austin said, "but there's plenty of room for a whole bunch of aliens."

He and Jerry had to look inside, squeezing past a fallen tree branch. They were gone only a few minutes when Austin scrambled back over the branch, his eyes wide.

"Madeline! There really is a dead body in here! Woo, it stinks!"

Jerry motioned to me. "You'd better come have a look, Mac. Austin, call nine-one-one."

"And I can lead them to the cave!"

Before I could mention that calling nine-one-one would lead the police to our location, Austin jumped on his four-wheeler and dashed off. Jerry used the flashlight on his phone to light my way in. Near the back of the cave was evidence of a cave in, a jumble of broken timbers and rocks, and crumpled in the middle was the body of a young woman with dark hair, lying on her side.

I bent down for a closer look, being careful not to touch the body. The woman wore a white blouse and a black skirt, the blouse torn and streaked with dirt. I took out my phone and compared the picture of Nadia Bill had given me to the pale bruised face of the young woman lying on the floor.

"This is Nadia Conrad," I said. "But why in the world was she here? And she wouldn't come in here and just die, would she?"

"Looks like bloodstains on her blouse," Jerry said.

And from what I could see, Nadia's hair was matted on one side. "She might have hit her head. Or someone else did."

Jerry moved his flashlight in a slow circle around Nadia's body. "There are plenty of rocks someone could use as a murder weapon."

I noticed something under her fingernails that looked like pieces of dark thread. What had she grasped in her efforts to stay alive? There was one small piece that had fallen from her hand, which I picked up and put in one of the plastic bags I carried.

Something else caught my eye. A small piece of paper lay in the dirt. Jerry had a better angle from his side, so I asked him to take a picture. Taking a small sample of thread was one thing, but I needed to leave the paper exactly where it was where the police could find it.

He took a picture and handed me his phone. I zoomed in to read what was written in black ink. "All secrets kept," it said. "All debts paid."

CHAPTER FIVE

P olice Chief Gus Brenner was a big man with short blond hair and small sharp blue eyes. He was not happy to find me and Jerry at the scene of what looked like a murder. He was not happy Austin was involved, and after thanking him for his help and giving him a stern lecture about going into the cave, sent him home. And he was especially not happy to discover the victim was Nadia Conrad. After checking out the crime scene, he returned to give Jerry and me one of his darkest frowns.

"What are you two doing here, Madeline?"

"Austin wanted us to see Carson's Crater and the cave," I said. "We found Nadia inside."

"Anything else?"

"There appear to be blood stains on her blouse and a possible head injury. There's a piece of paper on the ground. But why would she be in the cave?"

"The crater used to be a popular spot for kids to meet, and sometimes they'd go into the cave," the chief said, "but we've discouraged them from going in since the Thompson boy got killed seven years ago. We even had a barricade at one time, but as you can see, it's gone."

This incident must have been what Denisha's aunt was referring to when she warned the kids about going in the cave. "What happened to the Thompson boy?"

"As far as we can tell, he thought he'd explore, went too far, and the cave collapsed on him."

"Was there an investigation?" I asked, wondering if he had been attacked, as well.

"Yes. His death was ruled accidental. It wasn't the act of a serial cave killer, if that's what you're thinking."

Exactly what I was thinking until the Chief mentioned the time difference. "But it doesn't look like Nadia's death was an accident."

"No, I agree that it doesn't. But we'll need to wait for the medical examiner's report," he said.

I was encouraged by his use of "we." "So you're okay if I help with this case?" I asked.

"Any particular reason why?" he said, which was his standard answer.

That brought up the issue of Bill.

"Well," I began. If I didn't tell him now about Bill's relationship with Nadia as well as his relationship with me, he would throw me off the case the moment he found out. Which would be soon. "Nadia's employer is Bill Rosser, who is my ex-husband. She was a nanny for his three children. Bill had hired me to find her, because she didn't show up for work last week."

The Chief cocked an eyebrow, and said, "Thanks."

I waited in silence for the inevitable questions, but none came.

One of the other officers had already found the note and bagged it. He handed it to Chief Brenner who frowned as he read it. "'All secrets kept, all debts paid.' Any idea what this means,

Madeline?"

"No," I said, "but I'd like a chance to find out."

***

I called Bill the minute Jerry and I got into the Jeep.

"You've found her already?" he said. "Great news!"

"Not so great," I said. "I found her, but she's dead." In the shocked silence that followed, I said, "The police are going to have a word with you. You'd better have an alibi."

"You can't be serious!"

"This is very serious, Bill. You told me you were going to end the affair. Or maybe you lied and she was going to end the affair. You're the only one who knows. You see where this is going? Tell me again the last time you saw her."

"I can't believe you're asking me these questions."

"These are the same questions the police are going to ask. Right now you're dealing with me. When is the last time you saw her?"

Another long silence. When he answered, his voice was tight with anger. "I told you. I saw her on Sunday. We had our usual luncheon date. On Monday, we had a phone conversation and that's when she told me she was going to visit her grandfather and some friends in Celosia. Where did you find her?"

"In a local cave," I said.

"A cave? There are caves in Celosia? What the hell was she doing in a cave?"

I gave myself a slow count of five to remain calm. "I'm going to find out, but first, I need to make sure you're not involved. Where did you and Nadia meet for lunch?"

"At the Sheridan out by the Parkland airport."

"Can anyone at the restaurant vouch for you?" I asked.

His reply was scornful. "Of course they can. I'm there every Sunday."

Someone needed to invent an app that will let you reach through the phone and punch the person you're talking with. "So they all know a tall dark idiot who brings his much younger women to dine at the Sheridan every Sunday."

"Damn it, Madeline."

"Where is Tina every Sunday?"

"She takes the kids to visit her mother." He cleared his throat. "What happened to Nadia?"

"I don't know the official cause of death, but she may have been hit over the head with a rock."

"Good God, Madeline. You know I wouldn't do anything like that!"

"I know, Bill, but this is part of my investigation." For one thing, I needed to know the time of death before I asked Bill exactly where he was.

He took a long pause and then grumbled a few more curses under his breath. "Call me when you have some real information, Madeline. You can believe me or not, but I didn't have anything to do with Nadia's death."

He ended the call, and I sat staring at my phone. Didn't he understand that even though he was a cheat and a womanizer, I didn't want to believe he was capable of murder?

"What did Bill have to say?" Jerry asked, although I'm sure my expression told him everything.

"He saw Nadia Sunday afternoon at their weekly luncheon date while Tina visited her mother."

"How thoughtful."

"He's being very uncooperative, which isn't surprising. I'll know more once I find out how and when Nadia died."

"But that doesn't explain the mysterious note," Jerry said. "If she or her killer wrote it. 'All secrets kept, all debts paid.' As cryptic notes go, I give that one an A."

"And there's this." I pulled out the little baggie into which I had tucked the thread I'd found next to Nadia's body. It wasn't exactly a thread. It was thicker, more like a fiber, something you'd pull off a shirt. In the sunlight, I could tell it was dark blue.

As if my heart couldn't sink any lower. Dark blue. Navy blue. The color of Bill's favorite shirts.

***

Finding a body is always a shock, but knowing that someone you once loved and lived with could be seriously involved has its own shock value. I sat, wrapped up in my thoughts as Jerry drove us home. The bad news, of course, was that Nadia had undoubtedly been murdered. The encouraging news was Chief Brenner allowing me to help find her killer. I had to concentrate and not let my emotions get tangled up in this case.

Jerry hadn't said anything on the ride back, letting me work it out. When we got to the house, we sat in the Jeep, and he said, "Are you all right?"

"Yes," I said.

He looked at his watch. "I really need to find out what Fogarty's up to. I'm heading over to the theater to catch some of his lecture. I know you might not feel like going, so I can give you a full report."

I really didn't want to stay in the house alone with my gloomy thoughts. "You know what?" I said. "I think a talk on aliens would be the perfect distraction."

So Jerry turned the Jeep around and we went to the Celosia Little Theater for Professor Rodman Fogarty's lecture on Celosia's True Invasion.

***

Fogarty was tall and thin with black hair swept back from a high forehead. He was dressed in a black swallowtail coat, black striped trousers, and bright red ascot. He reminded me of a second rate magician. The crowd was small but enthusiastic. Jerry and I took seats half way down in the auditorium.

Fogarty began his talk with a discussion of how the pyramids lined up with the stars in the constellation Orion's belt, an incredible coincidence which proved beyond a shadow of a doubt that the ancient Egyptians had space travel. Then, using Power Point and a laser pointer, he indicated the glowing circles, bent grass, and burned ovals in the ground that proved UFOs had landed and taken off in the fields around Celosia. The photos had been taken in the Forties, however, and Fogarty informed us that since that time the circles and ovals had disappeared.

"No doubt covered up or destroyed by skeptics or people fearful of what they signified."

The next picture was of the crater. "Now I'm sure you all recognize Carson's Crater. This is obviously where a spaceship landed, and although there have been no traces found of the craft, I feel that a full investigation and excavation of the site would find amazing evidence of a failed alien invasion." He let this sink in. "Ladies and gentlemen, I am not here merely to lecture about the astounding coincidences between our constellations and possible alien life forms. I am here to spearhead this investigation and to find proof that will answer once and for all the question we all ask ourselves. Are we alone in the universe? My answer is no, and Celosia will lead the way in showing the world."

He talked for forty minutes, read passages from *True Invasion*, and then answered questions from the audience. Then he thanked everyone for coming. Several people stayed to say they'd be interested in helping him, and he took their contact information. When they left, Jerry and I approached the professor.

Fogarty gave a pleased start. "Jerry Fairweather, as I live and breathe! What in the world are you doing in town? I haven't stepped on any of your schemes, now, have I?"

Jerry shook his hand. "No, not at all. I live here now. This is my wife, Madeline Maclin. Mac, this is Rodman Fogarty."

He bowed. "Charmed, I'm sure. Jerry, my goodness, you are doing well for yourself in the marriage department, but then, you always landed on your feet. Do you ever see any of your old partners? Rick? Honor? What about Derek? You had quite a game going with him, as I recall."

"I'm out of the game now," Jerry said. "I work at Deely's Burger World in the mornings. Stop by and I'll give you a couple of bacon biscuits on the house."

Fogarty looked surprised. "Really? I'll certainly do that. Rusticating in the wilds, are you? Not what I expected from Big Mike's star pupil. Tell me, do you ever see or hear from Big Mike? I hope he's doing well."

"I haven't seen him in a long time," Jerry said. "I'm sure he's fine."

I could tell this was not the answer Fogarty wanted, but he quickly replaced his look of disappointment with a brief smile. "Yes, of course, he's always fine. I'd appreciate it if you ever do hear from him you'll let him know I am also doing fine."

"Be glad to," Jerry said.

"He always took a gratifying interest in my well-being, even after I left the game," Fogarty said. "I have never regretted leaving that world, though. A few close calls and I knew it was time to get out. Now I explore other worlds, and it is certainly more fulfilling. You'll join my investigating team, I trust?" He swung his dark gaze my way. "You, too, Madeline. I know we can discover what happened at Carson's Crater."

"Jerry will have more time to help out," I said. "I'm working on some cases at the moment."

"Mac runs a detective agency in town," Jerry said.

"Excellent! You must be interested in this mystery, then."

"It does sound intriguing," I said.

"Oh, it's beyond intriguing, my dear." Fogarty shook hands with us once more. "So glad to meet you, Madeline, and Jerry, I'll see you at Deely's in the morning."

As we walked up the aisle, I said, "I noticed you didn't tell Fogarty Big Mike was in Paris."

"I'm sure Rodman had nothing to do with the attempted coup, but why take a chance? Once a con man, always a con man." He realized his mistake. "Except me, of course. Totally reformed." He quickly changed the subject. "Tucker told me the Parkland Opera Company is doing *Aida* this December, full blown production, camels and everything. That was the first opera Harriet took us to when we were kids. We can't miss that."

Jerry's sister Harriet was aloof and prickly, but she was passionate about music and had instilled a love of opera in Jerry and his brothers. "There isn't an evil necklace in *Aida*, is there?" Jerry's operas often had a weird link to my cases. "What's that one about?"

"Standard opera stuff. Love, revenge, and death. Set in Egypt. Two women in love with the same man, and Aida and her lover get buried alive in a tomb."

"How did that happen?"

"Aida's a princess who has been captured by the Egyptians, and she falls in love with an Egyptian warrior named Radames. Unfortunately, Amneris, the Egyptian's king's daughter, is also in love with Radames, and Aida is her slave. Amneris knows about their love affair, and she is super jealous. That's pretty much all she sings about, how jealous she is."

"So she's the one who buries them alive?"

"No, Radames betrays his country and is condemned by the king. Aida just happens to be hiding out in the tomb waiting to die with him. Amneris is sorry about the whole thing—in a grand opera way."

"I get it. Nadia's the slave girl in love with Warrior Bill, and Tina's the jealous princess, who kills Nadia in the tomb-like cave, only I don't think Tina knows about the affair. Or maybe she does."

As we walked to my car, I said, "I can't believe this, but Nadia's murder is the seventh one I've been involved with since we moved to this little town."

"And the seventh murder you'll solve," Jerry said.

"I hope so," I said. "I just wish people would stop killing each other. Sometimes I wonder if the town motto should be 'Welcome to Celosia. Hope You Get Out Alive.'"

CHAPTER SIX

Tuesday morning, Jerry left some warm French toast in the oven for my breakfast and then revved up his Jeep to go to Deely's. I staggered down to the kitchen around eight and found a little note on the table from Denisha, reminding me her book signing was today from eleven till two. I'd have to be sure and stop by the book store. Not only was this a great opportunity for Denisha, but working with her and arranging the signing had helped pull our friend and local poet Hayden Amry out of a serious depression. I needed to support both of them.

I hadn't heard from Coreen Overmeyer. Apparently, the thrill of being interviewed for my YouTube channel wasn't as enticing as I'd hoped. I'd stop by her house later. And I needed to talk with Lon Forest.

But first, I needed to be fully awake. As soon as I was coherent, I called Chief Brenner to see if he had any details about Nadia's murder he could be convinced to tell me.

"Nadia died from blunt force trauma to the head and had been dead for two days," he said "From the angle of the blow, she was struck by an assailant."

I sincerely hoped Bill had an alibi for Saturday. "Definitely murder."

"Unfortunately, yes." His tone became even more serious. "Madeline, talk to me about Bill Rosser."

My heart sank. "Okay."

"You told me Nadia looked after his children, correct? And when she didn't come into work last week, he called you with his concerns."

"Yes, he actually came to my office."

"Your ex-husband is a person of interest, Madeline. When we searched Ms. Conrad's home, we found various holiday cards addressed to Nadia from 'Bill.' Also, the neighbors remember seeing a man matching his description visiting Ms. Conrad's apartment on several occasions. One neighbor recalled hearing part of a conversation where Ms. Conrad expressed concern about money, and Rosser was reported as saying, 'Don't worry about it.'"

This was getting worse and worse.

"You said Mr. Rosser hired you to find Nadia," the Chief said.

I'd never heard Chief Brenner speak so seriously. "Yes."

"And you did."

"And now he wants me to find out what happened."

The Chief gave a gusty sigh. "This is not a good idea, Madeline."

I could not believe Bill would kill anyone. "He's arrogant, thoughtless, and egotistical, but he's not a murderer. Do you have any suspects?"

"Not at this time."

"Thanks. I appreciate the information." I hung up before he could express further doubts.

My next call was to Bill. "Where were you last Saturday?"

His voice sounded smug. "You're a little late. I've already told the police where I was."

"Well, tell me."

Bill went through his weekend routine. He was up around nine Saturday to have breakfast and play golf all morning with his co-workers. Then the men had lunch at the club and played more golf. Bill had supper with Tina and the girls and then went out for drinks with some other buddies.

"Madeline, I'm sorry about Nadia, I really am, but there's no way I was in Celosia Saturday."

I felt a rush of relief. I never wanted to believe he had anything to do with murder—but a tiny part of my investigator's brain still wondered if he could be lying.

"Let me have the names and phone numbers of those friends."

"Damn it, Madeline."

"It's my job," I said. "You hired me to find Nadia, and I did. You are now a person of interest in her murder investigation." I let that sink in. "Do you want me to find Nadia's killer and clear your name?"

"Yes," he growled.

"Okay, then."

He gave me the names and phone numbers of the friends he'd been with Saturday night. "Is that all?"

"Actually, no," I said. "Were you really planning to break it off with her?"

"Does it matter?"

"At this point, everything matters, Bill." I needed to know what her frame of mind was. Why she took off.

"Look, Madeline. I treated her well, if that's what you're asking. I don't want to sound like a jerk, but she fell for me hard. She was from Celosia, and this was her first time in the big city."

"People from Celosia are not rural hicks, Bill." I wanted to say Nadia wasn't some innocent flower. She had a conscience.

"Yeah, okay, sorry."

"So if she'd said, 'I want to break it off,' that would have been okay with you?"

"Of course. I wouldn't have forced her. I don't do that with any woman."

He didn't add, because I can always get another woman, but I knew from experience that's what he meant. "What did you talk about during your Sunday lunches? Did she ever discuss her life and her friends in Celosia?"

"No, she liked hearing about my life and my friends."

Which I'm sure he made sound wonderful and exciting. "No doubt she hung on your every word and agreed with every opinion."

"Sure, at first," he said, sounding offended. "The last time we met she was more reserved. I asked her what was wrong—I felt protective of her, you know—but she just said she had to take care of business in Celosia."

"What business?" I said.

"I didn't ask. I respected her privacy."

I bet.

I'd had enough of Bill. "I'll talk to you later," I said. I ended the call and set to work calling the numbers Bill had given me. All of his friends confirmed Bill had been with them Saturday night at the Starlight Bar. I sat back in my chair, only slightly satisfied with the results. What if Bill had asked them to lie for him? I was not usually this suspicious, but I knew my ex. I needed to find absolute proof he was not in Celosia that night.

I was on my third cup of coffee when our handywoman Nell

Brenner's white van drove around the house. Nell got out and knocked on the back door.

"Morning, Madeline. Sad news about Nadia, isn't it?"

"Yes," I said. "Come on in. There's French toast and coffee if you'd like breakfast."

"Wouldn't mind a cup of coffee." She fixed a cup and sat down across from me at the table. Nell was large and blond like her father and had his small sharp blue eyes. She was dressed as usual in her white paint-splattered overalls and cap. She took off her cap for a moment to push back a stray lock of hair before replacing the cap snugly and pulling her ponytail through the back. "Guess you've already talked to Dad."

I handed her a cup of coffee. "Just a short while ago."

"So he's letting you in on the case?"

"Not officially."

"Had to be a random attack," Nell said. "I can't imagine it was somebody she knew—unless—"

"Unless what?"

She took a drink of coffee and set her cup down. "Have you found Juniper's necklace yet?"

I could see where this was going. "Nell, I don't think Nadia was attacked by an alien necklace."

"I told you it was cursed, Madeline. That's the only possible explanation. You'd better find it before it strikes again."

"Well, unless it was able to pick up a heavy object and hit Nadia, I don't believe it's dangerous."

She took another sip and considered my argument. "It could have used its alien power to make the killer do it."

Alien Necklace Mind Control. Perfect. "I'll look into that," I said.

This satisfied Nell, and as soon as she finished her coffee and left, I decided I'd better get my investigation into high gear before this case got any nuttier.

***

At Deely's, I joined the Geezer Club. Horace Stanly, Nell's great uncle, was a large distinguished-looking man with an impressive silver moustache. Frank Odum was a thin lanky fellow. R.W. Jessup was the smallest of the three. His round head and little features always made me think of a potato. The men wore striped short-sleeved shirts under overalls. Horace wore a yellow and green John Deere cap. Frank's cap was dark blue with a Navy insignia. R.W.'s was black and decorated with a large green fish. All three touched the brims of their caps as I slid into the booth beside Horace.

"To what do we owe the honor, Madeline?" Frank asked.

"Looking for information, as always."

"Watcha workin' on now?"

"Nadia Conrad's murder."

All three men looked upset. "Oh, yes, Albert's granddaughter," Frank said. "We're going out to see about him today. That's a damn shame, that is."

"More than a shame," Horace said. "Things like that shouldn't happen around here. Hope you can find whoever did it."

"I plan to," I said. "She was in town last week. Did any of you happen to see her?"

"Came in Tuesday at lunchtime, didn't she?" Frank said.

"No, it was Wednesday," R.W. said.

"Could've sworn it was Tuesday."

"Wednesday," R.W. said firmly. "She and Lon Forest sat right over there in that booth."

"Two high school friends catching up?" I asked. "A friendly conversation?"

"Yeah, they talked quite a bit."

"I guess it was friendly," Frank said. "Didn't pay too much attention."

"Didn't look friendly to me," R.W. said.

"Yes, it was. They was holding hands."

"And she pulled hers away."

"Because she was getting ready to leave," Frank said, annoyed. "Don't mind him, Madeline. She came over and spoke to us before she left, smiling and polite, like always." He looked down at his coffee cup and gave a sad sigh. "Guess that was the last time we saw her."

Frank took out his handkerchief and took a quick swipe at his eyes before he blew his nose. Horace cleared his throat.

"Who else might she have visited besides Lon and her grandfather?" I asked.

"Used to come into Deely's with that Thompson boy, didn't she?" R.W. asked his friends.

"Patrick Thompson?" I asked. "Is he still in town?"

"Lord, no," Horace said. "Had a bad accident back when they were in high school. Went fooling around in Carson's Cave, and the roof fell in."

"No, that's not what happened," R.W. said. "One of those timbers holding up the roof gave way."

"You're both wrong," Frank said. "The way I heard it, there was drugs involved. The kids used to ride out to Carson's Crater and Carson's Cave to fool around with each other, and you know some of them had drugs."

Horace disagreed. "I don't ever hear tell of there being any drugs. Nobody figured out exactly what happened."

I let the fellows argue. When they ran out of theories, I said,

"Well, there's something else I need to ask you gentlemen about, you especially, R.W.," I said. "It's about the UFO you saw when you were a little boy."

The other men guffawed. R.W. scowled at them, or scowled as well as his little features would allow. "That damn story just won't quit. Bad enough these two used to call me 'Space Boy.'"

"But you did see something?"

"That story's not worth repeating," he said. "And now this Fogarty character's stirring things up again."

Right on cue, Rodman Fogarty came into Deely's—or started to. His way was blocked by three very large young men in jeans and tee shirts, one of whom bumped him. From where I was sitting, it looked like an accident, but Fogarty took offense, and words were exchanged. Two of the men held the third one back. Fogarty marched into the diner, muttering under his breath, and took a seat on one of the stools at the counter.

The men glowered at him and came to the Geezer Club corner.

"Didn't I teach you boys better manners?" R.W. said testily.

"We were there first," one said. Up close, all three young men had R.W.'s small features and his trademark scowl, but they were much bigger than their father, with muscular shoulders and legs and very little neck.

R.W. continued to scold. "You start a fist fight on the street and you won't be coming to town. And why are you in town? You've got plenty to do on the farm."

"Just wanted breakfast," another said.

"Well, get some breakfast to go and move on. That back field better be mowed by the time I get home. Sorry about the disturbance, Madeline. These boys of mine ain't got a lick of sense sometimes."

The three men exchanged glances but didn't argue. They lumbered to the counter and sat down a few stools away from Fogarty.

Jerry had seen the altercation. He came out to smooth things over. "Morning, Rod. Hi, fellas. Everybody want bacon biscuits?"

"We gotta have ours to go, Jerry," one of R.W.'s boys said. "Four each and some fries if you've got them ready."

"They'll be ready," he said.

"I will need some strong black coffee with mine," Fogarty said in a lofty tone. "I did not expect to be accosted by provincial oafs this morning."

This was an amazingly stupid thing to say with three behemoths sitting within smacking range, but fortunately for Fogarty, the behemoths' dad was watching them, and they didn't rise to the bait.

Horace tipped his chin up in Fogarty's direction. "This fella a friend of Jerry's?"

"Yes, unfortunately," I said.

"He knows a lot of mighty odd people."

That was one way of putting it.

I thanked the men for their help and walked up to the counter. Jerry had wisely fixed the Jessup boys' order first. As they paid, I heard him say, "I'll take care of it." They shouldered past Fogarty's stool at the counter, getting as close as they could without touching him. Fogarty ignored them. As soon as they were gone, he stood up and made a bow.

"Good morning, Madeline. So nice to see you again. I'm leading an expedition out to Carson's Crater this morning. I'd love for you to join us."

"That sounds interesting," I said. "When are you going?"

"Ten thirty, accompanied by several interested citizens."

"I can't join your group today," I said. "Possibly another time."

"Not to worry. I'm sure I'll make several trips out to investigate the crater." He sat back down and motioned for me to take the stool next to his. He lowered his voice. "Now tell me, do you assist Jerry with his little projects?"

"He really doesn't have any. Not the kind you're referring to, that is."

He waved this away. "Oh, I'm not sure I believe that. It's very difficult to walk away from that life. Trust me, I know. He's still a young man. I can see him aspiring to Big Mike's position, should Big Mike ever step down."

Another mention of Big Mike. Rodman Fogarty was definitely angling for information. "Actually, it's the other way around," I said, keeping my voice light. "Jerry assists me with my little projects. You wouldn't guess, but there's enough excitement in this town to keep us busy."

Fogarty started to reply when Jerry arrived with his bacon biscuits and a cup of coffee. "Here you go. Heading out to the crater today?"

"I am, indeed," he said. "I hope your lovely wife will find time in her busy schedule to join me."

At Jerry's practiced look of inquiry, I said, "I have another engagement. I'll let you know if I find anything useful. Are you going exploring with Mr. Fogarty?"

"Rodman, please, dear lady," Fogarty said.

"Yeah, I'd like to find out more about the UFO," Jerry said.

"Excellent," Fogarty said, his mouth full of biscuit. "And speaking of excellent, these biscuits are delicious."

***

I left Fogarty extolling the virtues of the bacon biscuit and went to my car where I accessed the online archives of the Celosia News and searched for Patrick Thompson and the year he graduated from high school, seven years ago. The headline for the article said, 'Local Teen Killed in Cave-in.' Patrick's photo showed a handsome young man, dark-haired and dark-eyed with a devil may care expression. His death had occurred on September 17 and was ruled accidental.

Nadia had been murdered last Saturday, September 17.

My pondering was interrupted when Fogarty came out of Deely's, got into his car, and drove away. Next, Jerry exited the diner, hopped into his Jeep, and followed Fogarty. I searched further for more information about Patrick's fatal accident, but other than his obituary, there was nothing.

But I did have two more of Nadia's friends to interview.

CHAPTER SEVEN

A wide, unkempt yard separated Lon Forest's house from Juniper's on Heritage Lane. In contrast to Juniper's, Lon's house was a small brick structure with a garage on one side and a screened-in porch on the other. An older model beige Oldsmobile with a dented back bumper sat in the garage. As I went up the walk, the elderly woman sitting on the porch waved to me and pushed the fat black cat out of her lap. She used her cane to stand and let me in.

Her dark eyes peered at me through thick oversized glasses. "Is that Madeline Maclin?"

"Yes," I said. "You're Loraine Forest, right?" She was a tiny woman with a sharp little nose and short silver hair. Of course, I thought. Kathy Holly had told me Lon lived with his mother, but I hadn't made the connection until now. I'd met Loraine through the Women's Improvement Society, but her health issues prevented her from taking part in their projects.

"Come in and have a seat," she said. She settled back into her small rocking chair. "What brings you to the neighborhood today? You must be trying to find out who killed that poor girl."

"Yes, I am," I said.

"You'll have to speak up, dear. I don't have on my hearing aids this morning. They're a darned nuisance. Would you like some tea? Shoo, Roger. Madeline doesn't want your hair all over her."

The cat ignored her and wound about my legs as if attempting to rub off as much fur as he could. He had bright green eyes that matched the glimpses of green collar I could see through his thick black fur. "No, thanks," I said, pitching my voice a little louder. I sat down in another rocking chair. "I'd like to ask you some questions, though."

"Oh, my, yes. I'd love to be part of an investigation. Roger, no. Come here." She pulled the cat into her lap. Roger immediately hopped off and went to the porch door. "No, you are not going out." He plopped down, offended. "Such a baby." She gave me an owl-like stare from her huge glasses. "What did you want to ask me, Madeline?"

"Nadia was in Celosia last week to visit her grandfather," I said. "Did she come visit you?"

Loraine took such a long moment to answer I thought perhaps her memory was failing. "No, I haven't seen her in a long while, not since she and Lonny were in high school together. Maybe Lonny saw her." She leaned back in her chair and called into the house. "Lonny! Would you come out here, please?"

A tall young man came out to the porch. His dark hair was neatly combed, and he had a crop of stylish stubble. I could see by his dark eyes and the shape of his nose he was definitely related to Loraine. He wore jeans and a tee shirt with the logo from the Iron Man movie. He spoke loudly but politely to Loraine. "Did you need something, Mom?"

"This is Madeline Maclin, the detective," Loraine said. "She's trying to find out what happened to Nadia Conrad."

At the mention of Nadia's name, he swallowed a sob. "God, that was awful. Do the police have any idea who killed her?"

"Not yet," I said. "When's the last time you saw her?"

He sat down in another rocking chair and rubbed his face. "Last Wednesday. We met at Deely's and talked about old times."

I recalled how R.W. didn't think their conversation was particularly friendly. "Did she seem anxious or upset about anything?"

"No. She stopped by to see me and Coreen—and her grandfather, of course."

I recalled how annoyed another friend had been that Nadia didn't call or come by to visit her. "Not Kathy Holly?"

Lon made an exasperated sound. "I doubt it. Kathy always thought she was part of our group, but she pushed her way in. Have you already talked to her? Did she give you the impression I was some creepy kid still living with my mother?"

"Not the creepy part, but I did get that sort of vibe."

"Well, it's true I live here. I'm Mom's caretaker."

"Just can't get around like I used to," Loraine said. "Can't see without these heavy glasses. Can't hear without those itchy hearing aids."

"I told you we'd see about getting some new ones," Lonny said.

"Don't really want any," she said. "And you keep saying you'll take me to play Bingo at Betty's place. I haven't been one time."

He grinned as if he were used to her complaints. "I'll take you sometime soon, I promise. Madeline, I will freely admit living here saves me money. I'm working on my Masters degree at Parkland Community College."

"Lonny's going to be a chiropractor," Loraine said.

"Biologist, Mom."

Loraine reached over to pat his hand. "It took him a while to find his path, but now he's on his way. I don't know what I would've done without him. I've always been in poor health, and it's a blessing to have him around. But poor sweet Nadia! I can't believe she's gone."

Roger gave an aggrieved yowl, and Loraine sighed. "Oh, all right. Would you reach over and let him out, please, Madeline?" I gave the screen door a push, and Roger slid out.

"Lonny, watch him and make sure he doesn't get in Juniper's yard." She turned to me. "Juniper hates Roger. She doesn't want him anywhere near her cat. Throws things at him and squirts him with the hose. And one time she had the nerve to spray some nasty smelling stuff on him. Thought I'd never get it out of his fur."

"I'm watching, Mom," Lon said.

"Don't know what makes her so ornery."

Lon gave me a look that suggested he'd heard this complaint many times. "This high school group of yours," I said to him. "What's the story there?"

Up to now, Lon Forest had been open and willing to talk, but now I noticed a definite change in his manner. He stood. "Mom, I'd like to show Madeline your roses. We'll be right back."

"Oh, by all means, go ahead," she said.

Lon opened the screen door for me, and we walked around the house to a small garden where a fat rose bush filled with red blossoms and buds spread between two maple trees.

"Sorry if I was a bit short just then," he said. "It's very difficult to talk about Nadia."

"I understand," I said. "It must have been quite a shock to hear she'd been found in Carson's Cave."

His gaze was on the rose bush. "Yes, it was."

"I understand that before it caved in, the cave used to be a meeting place for teens."

He gave a slight flinch. "No, we hung out at the crater. I was always trying to impress everyone with tales about UFOs and aliens landing in the crater. I really believed all that stuff then. I was quite the nerd."

"So perhaps Nadia decided to visit the crater for old times' sake?"

"Maybe. I haven't been out there in years, and I know Coreen hasn't. She's way too busy with her garden life."

"Do you have any idea why Nadia would have gone to the cave?"

He shook his head.

"When you met at Deely's I imagine she had a lot to tell you about life in Parkland."

He toyed with one of the roses. "Yeah, the usual. It's all good."

Was it all good? Or had Nadia confided in her old high school pal about her flirtation with the boss? Lon was hesitant to offer any more details.

"Did she have any plans for the future?" I asked. "Maybe a Home Helper type business of her own?"

"No. She would've told me if she did."

"So no secrets between old friends, right?"

Lon gave a start. "Ow! Thorn got me," he said and briefly sucked his finger. "Stupid roses. Sorry, Madeline. Didn't mean to startle you."

"That's okay," I said, wondering if it was the thorn or the word "secret" that surprised him.

I told Lon I had to meet with another client, and we circled back around to the porch to say good-by to Loraine.

"So nice to see you, Madeline," she said. "You come by any time. Lonny, there's money on the kitchen table. You go ahead and get me those hearing aids."

"Sure thing, Mom." Lon shook my hand. "I really appreciate you investigating Nadia's murder."

"I'll do everything I can," I thanked them again and asked if they recalled anything else to call me.

***

Next, I drove to Coreen Overmeyer's house in the rarefied community of Silver Lakes, an upscale development at Celosia's town limit. All the houses looked like gray and white mini-cathedrals. Coreen's was the largest, taking up the entire end of a cul-de-sac. The landscaping was flawless, every little bush and tree sculpted and arranged in neat patterns. No surprise there. The huge glass-paneled front door was flanked by giant marble urns filled with flowing pink petunias.

I parked out front, went up the curved sidewalk to the door, and rang the doorbell, which set off a series of echoing chimes within the house. I expected a butler or maid to answer, but no one came to the door. I tried again and decided Coreen Overmeyer either wasn't at home or was just avoiding me.

I gave her another call and this time when I heard her voicemail say "creator of the Overmeyer Prestige rose," I had an idea. I ended the call and called Tucker.

"First of all, congratulations on Lillian," I said when he answered. "Jerry showed me the picture, and it's gorgeous."

"Thanks very much," he said.

"Second, do you know Coreen Overmeyer, creator of the

Overmeyer Prestige rose?"

He chuckled. "Oh, everyone in the rose world knows Coreen. She's somewhat of a diva."

"I need to get in touch with her, but she's not answering my calls or answering her doorbell. Any ideas?"

"Well, she has three homes, so she's probably out of town."

"Three homes? Each one more spectacular than the last?"

"I've only been to the one in Celosia, so I can't say for sure, but I imagine that's true," he said. "Your best bet is to attend their next meeting, which will be—hang on, let me check—tomorrow at ten at her Silver Lakes residence."

"That's where I am right now," I said. "It's really lovely in an overblown sort of way."

"That pretty much describes Coreen."

"How well do you know her?" I asked.

"I don't know anything about her personal life," Tucker said. "I know a lot about her gardening techniques, though, and her Prestige rose because that's all she talks about at flower shows."

I had another idea. "Have you been to any of the Celosia Garden Club meetings?"

"A couple," he said.

At this point, Jerry would've said something like, "So you need a way in?" but since Tucker was not as devious as his older brother, I had to be the one to suggest it. "Would you be willing to attend tomorrow's meeting and bring me along as a guest?"

"Of course," he said. "Some of the people there always have questions about proper spacing for Ramblers and Climbers."

Trusting that Ramblers and Climbers were names for more athletic roses, I said, "Okay, thanks. I'll meet you at Coreen's tomorrow at ten."

***

Denisha's book signing ended at two, and it was past one o'clock. Just enough time to grab a quick bite of lunch and get to the book store. I sent Jerry a text to let him know I was on my way.

"Meet you there," he replied.

Georgia's Books was on Main Street, one of the few remaining independent book stores in the area. A colorful sign on the window said, "Book Signing Today. Meet the Author, Denisha Simpson." Stacks of Denisha's little poetry book were displayed in the window. Denisha was seated at the front of the store at a table full of more books. She had on a fancy pink dress and instead of having her hair in rows and beads, she wore her natural curls tied back with a wide pink ribbon. She beamed at me.

"I knew you'd come."

"I wouldn't miss it," I said. "How are sales going?"

"I've sold ten so far." She handed me a copy. "This one's yours. I've already signed it." As I reached for my wallet, she said, "No, it's a gift. I wouldn't have met Hayden if you didn't have him staying at your house that day, and he wouldn't have met me or known that I write poetry, and this whole thing might have never happened."

The poetry book was white with a design of pink and yellow flowers with the title, *Bright Thoughts* by Denisha Simpson, appearing to grow out of the blossoms. It was a lovely little book. Hayden had made every effort to ensure it looked as professional as possible. "Thank you. Where is Hayden?"

"He's right there talking to Georgia."

Georgia and Hayden stood at the counter in the center of the store. The owner of Georgia's Books, Georgia Taylor, was a slim, efficient woman in her sixties. She had auburn tinted hair and wore a pair of half glasses on a pearl necklace. Hayden Amry was a handsome young man with light brown hair and blue green eyes the color of a tropical ocean. He held his raggedy little white dog, Felicity, nestled under one arm, and she gazed up at him adoringly. Her tail wagged as I approached.

"Looks like the book signing is a success," I said.

"Denisha's so excited," Georgia said. "And I have to say, her poems are very good. Almost as good as yours, Hayden, and a bit more understandable."

He smiled. "I'm working on that."

I noticed copies of Fogarty's *True Invasion* displayed by the register. "Have you sold many of those?"

"Quite a few," Georgia said. "He's stirred up a bit of excitement around town."

"Jerry went out with him this morning to hunt for UFOs," I said.

Up went her auburn eyebrows. "Oh, do they know each other?"

"I'm afraid so."

"You didn't go with them? I would think a UFO landing near Celosia would be a good mystery to solve."

"There's another mystery I'm investigating," I said. "Nadia Conrad."

Hayden shifted Felicity to his other arm. "That was awful news, Madeline. Are you on the case?"

"Yes, I am," I said.

"I didn't know her. I may have seen her a time or two."

"A lovely person," Georgia said. "She and her friends used to come in here often. I was truly saddened to hear about her death. Do the police have any suspects?"

My idiot of an ex-husband, I wanted to say. "They're doing all they can. Did she stop by the store last week?"

"Yes, she did. She wanted to know if I still carried *Sky Watchers Monthly*, and I was happy to tell her I did. That was always one of her favorite magazines."

"Do you have another copy?" I asked.

"Right over here."

Sky Watchers Monthly was mainly concerned with stars, constellations, and planets, but there was a column titled "UFO Corner." Looked like Lon wasn't the only one who was interested in aliens.

Jerry came in, admired Denisha's display, and told her he needed five copies to send to his friends.

"I know all about your friends," she said. "You sure they read poetry?"

"They'll read yours if I tell them to. Be sure to sign them."

After she signed her books, he brought them to the counter to pay. "Good morning, everybody. Hello, Felicity." The little dog wriggled excitedly as he patted her head. "How's she working out, Hayden?"

"She's the best. The only problem is she wants to sleep between me and Shana. Shana's not having any of that. And Felicity likes to roll on the comforter, so there are all these little white hairs everywhere."

"Get Felicity a little pal to roll with."

"I've thought about it," he said. "Find any aliens?"

"Only Fogarty. He's absolutely convinced a UFO made Carson's Crater, and quite a few Celosian citizens agree with him."

Georgia rang up Jerry's books and took his money. "That's not any crazier than Mantis Man," she said, referring to Celosia's resident monster, a mutant insect that supposedly lived in the woods. Jerry and I had already had an encounter with the mantis.

"Or SkinkFest," Hayden said. "Maybe the aliens are giant skinks."

She put the books in a bag and handed them to Jerry. "Who knows? Maybe it will bring more tourists to town."

"Or run them off," Jerry said. "Not everyone likes the idea of being abducted by aliens."

"Did that happen, too?" she asked.

"According to Fogarty, several local farmers were taken up into the mother ship."

"Oh, that old nonsense. I wouldn't bother with that," she said and left to assist customers looking for the children's books.

"Did you find out anything else?" I asked Jerry.

"I could bore you with the entire history of close encounters in North Carolina, but let's save that for another time."

We stayed for a while and watched as proudly as parents while Denisha greeted her friends and fans. Hayden sat next to her, Felicity in his lap, and opened the books for her to sign, smiling and relaxed, a far cry from the disoriented and listless young man we'd seen last month. Then we told Denisha congratulations once more and left the store.

"How was your morning?" Jerry asked as we walked back to our cars.

"I talked with Juniper's neighbors, Loraine and Lon Forest. Lon seems pretty upset by Nadia's death. I'm going to see Coreen Overmeyer at the Garden Club meeting tomorrow. And since Tucker's the rose expert and Coreen is the queen, he's going undercover with me."

Jerry chuckled. "That ought to be good."

"Do you want to come?"

"To the Garden Club? Nope."

Jerry's Jeep was parked across the street from my Mazda. Overhead, a man high up in a cherry picker attached a bright yellow banner to a telephone pole. The banner, proclaiming the Twenty-Fifth Annual SkinkFest, was decorated with skinks hoisting large striped mugs and eating hot dogs.

"I can't wait until Friday," Jerry said. "Me and the skinks are going to paint this town red—or blue, I guess."

I slid into the passenger's seat, frowning in thought. Why would Nadia or any of her friends return to Carson's Cave? Would they gather for some sort of memorial? Wouldn't they go to his grave, instead? I frowned until Jerry said, "What are you thinking?"

"Just trying to figure out why Nadia would have been in the cave," I said. "And there's the coincidence of Patrick and Nadia's deaths being on September 17. Does that date have special significance for the friends?"

"Well, if they went to the cave to remember Patrick, that doesn't explain why Nadia was killed."

"I can't think of any other reason she would have gone there." I sighed and changed the subject. "Did Fogarty find anything at the crater today?"

"He collected soil and plant samples, filled his sample bags with rocks, and declared the outing a success."

"Speaking of samples, I want to express my sympathies to Nadia's grandfather—and get a sample of her handwriting. I also want to get one of Bill's dark blue shirts and check out the fiber I found."

"Which one first?" Jerry asked. "If we're going to Parkland, I'd like to stop by Pot Luck Alley and see if Willow knows what Fogarty's up to."

"Parkland first," I said. "Ever since I found that fiber, I've been dreading to know where it came from."

"You think Bill's going to hand over one of his shirts?"

"He'd damn well better," I said.

CHAPTER EIGHT

We decided to take Jerry's Jeep to Parkland, and all the way my mind skittered from one awful possibility to another. Was Bill crafty enough to pretend to care about Nadia while plotting her murder? Had Nadia threatened to tell Tina about their alleged affair? Had Bill grown tired of Nadia and wanted her out his life permanently?

I was jarred back to reality when Jerry honked his horn at a minivan that pulled out in front of the Jeep.

He glanced my way. "You okay?"

"I don't know. I keep thinking of so many ways this whole case could go wrong. I mean, what if Bill really—?" I couldn't say the rest.

"Mac, you lived with the man for what, two years?"

"Yes, but you've been involved with all my murder cases in Celosia. You've seen how crazy people can be, what they'll do for love or money or revenge. I'm beginning to believe anyone can snap."

"So what's Bill's motive? He doesn't have any trouble finding love, or at least sex, that's for sure. He's rich, so he doesn't need money. Maybe it's revenge. You'll have to ask him about that."

"Oh, I will," I said.

Jerry said the only reason he'd want to see Bill was to punch him in the nose, so I dropped him off at the pawn shop in Pot Luck Alley. By the time I'd reached Bill's house, I was ready for anything.

Except Tina.

She met me at the door. "Come in, Madeline. I want to talk to you."

She led me through a huge foyer filled with plants in expensive-looking vases and spindly little chairs with decorative cushions to a vast sun room overlooking an immaculately trimmed yard. She indicated a plush chair in a pattern of yellow and gray flowers and took the matching chair opposite me. The shy, petite blond Tina I'd met before had barely said hello. This Tina was still petite and blond, but had plenty to say.

"Now then," she said in a firm, un-Tina-like voice. "The children are at their grandmother's. Bill is playing golf, or so he says. Nadia is dead, so he'll have to find another girlfriend. I want to know what you know and what he's told you. Then I'm going to decide what to do."

Okay. So she knew everything. I decided I needed her help, and maybe we could get Bill out of this mess. "All right," I said. "Here's what I know. Bill told me he and Nadia were having an affair. She asked him if she could have a few days off to go to Celosia to visit friends."

"That's right."

"But when he hadn't heard from her by the weekend, he got worried. He came to see me Monday, and hired me to find her. I did find her in a local cave. She'd been attacked and hit on the head."

Tina went pale. "He didn't tell me all that."

"The Celosia police consider Bill a person of interest. Bill told me he had an alibi for last Saturday night, the night Nadia was murdered, but I have to be sure. I've come to Parkland to get one of his dark blue shirts."

"One of his shirts? Why would you need that?"

"There were some dark blue fibers under Nadia's fingernails. I sincerely hope they don't match the fibers in Bill's shirts."

I thought for a moment she might faint. She grasped the arms of her chair. "Oh, my God. What if they do?"

"Then I'll find another explanation." Unfortunately, the only other explanation I could think of involved a passionate night of tearing off clothes. I didn't say this to Tina.

"I see." She sat still for a long moment. Her voice trembled. "Dear God. Poor Nadia. She didn't deserve that. No one does."

"How long had you known about the affair?" I asked quietly.

She looked down at her rings. The wedding band was gold and engraved with silver swirls. The style of her engagement ring was too large for her small hand, but I'm sure Bill had chosen it for the three fat diamonds. "About a year ago, when she first came to work for us. The trouble is, I liked Nadia and so did the children. I don't think she meant to hurt me. Bill probably gave her money."

"Did you ever confront him?"

"No. This may sound cold, but I wanted to watch and see what happened before I decided what to do."

"Do you still love him?"

She blinked as if holding back tears. "Of course. I don't understand why he feels the need to cheat, but I still love him. You know, don't you, Madeline?"

"I don't love him anymore," I said. "He's not the best man in the world, but I don't think he's a murderer."

"Me, either," she said. "What else can I do?"

I took out my phone. "These are the people Bill said he was with last Saturday night. I called them, and they corroborated his story."

She read through the names. "I recognize most of them as his golfing buddies. They'd be likely to cover for him, but not something this serious. Not when the police are involved. These men are prominent business men in Parkland. It's doubtful they'd risk their jobs and reputations for Bill." She looked at me, her expression hopeful. "Do you think you can find the real murderer?"

"I'm going to try, but Bill's going to have to cooperate."

She stood. "Let me get one of his shirts."

She was back in a few minutes. I took the shirt and thanked her.

"I hope you can find the person who did this," she said. "In spite of everything, I really liked Nadia. I know the affair had to be Bill's idea, and she just couldn't resist."

Yep, good old irresistible Bill. "If he's playing golf, where would he be?"

"Mason Country Club. It's his favorite. If he's playing golf. But he's probably at Rocko's. That's the new bar downtown near the park. You have his number, don't you?"

Oh, I had his number, all right.

***

As Tina and I both suspected, Bill was not playing golf at Mason Country Club but chatting with the waitresses at Rocko's. I knew this because I could hear them giggling over the music in the background over the phone. I sighed and sat back in the Jeep.

"Okay, ladies, I have to take this call," he said. "Madeline, I hope you have good news for me."

"Not so good news for you," I said. "Tina knows all about your idiotic behavior."

"What?" he said. "Did you tell her?"

"No, she figured it out for herself."

"That's impossible." He spoke to the waitresses. "Excuse me, ladies. I need to take this outside." His voice when he returned to me was terse. "There is no way she could've known."

"Oh, for heaven's sake, she isn't stupid. No, wait. Maybe she is. She says she still loves you. She wants me to help you, so I think you should go home right now, confess everything, beg her forgiveness, and do whatever she says, because in spite of everything, she will forgive you, and she will come visit you in prison every day."

After a long pause where I could almost hear Bill's teeth grinding, he said, "This isn't funny."

"No, it's sad," I said. "It's sad that you lied about going to play golf today—that you'd even consider playing golf—and instead you're partying with other women while Tina is at home worried sick about you. It really makes me wonder what else you've lied about."

His voice was defensive. "It's not like that."

"Then tell me what it's like."

"I can't talk right now, Madeline. I'll call you later."

He ended the call. I stared at my phone in disbelief. "I'll call you later"? What was he thinking? It was already too late.

***

When I pulled up in front of the pawn shop in Pot Luck Alley, Jerry was standing outside, talking with a young blond woman dressed in black jeans and a black tee shirt. They came to the passenger side of the Jeep.

"Mac, you remember Willow," Jerry said.

"Yes, of course," I said. I'd met Willow during one of Jerry's cons that went slightly awry. She was in her thirties, but looked like a Goth teenager, complete with black fingernails, silver skull ring, and silver earrings in the shape of bats.

"Willow's been giving me an update on Fogarty," Jerry said.

"Got careless on his last con and spent five years in prison," Willow said.

That was unexpected. "So that's why he said he'd left Con World."

Willow chuckled. "Con World. That's a good one. Yeah, he really left. He was lucky to only serve five years. Usually the sentence for fraud can be as much as twenty."

"What did he do?" I asked.

"I think he was running roof and drive fixings down in Florida. You know, where you promise someone you'll fix their roof or driveway, but you take the money and run. But he'd really like to find out who ratted on him. He came by here the other day, asking if I knew, but I never had any dealings with him."

"Didn't he work with Sawbuck Sam?" Jerry asked.

"For a while. But mostly he was a solo act."

I had my concerns. "Is he a threat to Jerry, or Big Mike, or has he really gone over the edge with the UFO stuff?"

"He's always been a bit out there," Willow said, "but he's a full-on alien hunter now."

"Sure you don't want to come to Celosia and catch some flying saucers?" Jerry asked her.

"No, thanks," she said. "It's my turn to mind the shop."

"Mac, show her the picture of Juniper's necklace," he said. "Maybe somebody will pawn it."

Willow took a close look at the photo. "So this is the alien artifact? Nice," she said. "I'll check around the other shops in the area."

Jerry got in the passenger seat and waved good-by. He clicked on his seat belt. "How did things go with Tina?" he asked. "Did she let you have one of Bill's shirts?"

"Not only that, she knew about Bill's affair with Nadia. When I told her he was a person of interest in her murder, she still plans to stand by her man. Her man, by the way, did not believe she knew anything and said he'd call me later. I don't understand why he's being so evasive."

"Hiding something? Another woman, perhaps?"

"Good lord, I hope not."

Jerry grinned. "Bill, the gift that keeps on giving."

***

On our way back to Parkland, we stopped at the Conrad farm. Mr. Conrad was sitting on his porch. He lifted a hand in greeting. The hound dog beside him lifted its head and barked a half-hearted warning.

As Jerry and I walked to the porch, Mr. Conrad slowly pulled himself up.

"Mr. Conrad, I'm so sorry about Nadia," I said, and Jerry offered his sympathies, as well.

He appeared more frail than before, his eyes wet with tears. "Thank you," he said. "I been hearing all kinds of things about what happened. Figured you'd know the truth."

"I wish I knew the whole truth," I said.

He squinted up at me. "Thought about calling since you left me your card and all, but I just couldn't seem to find the energy. Police came by and talked to me, but they didn't act like they knew who might have done it. What about this man she was working for? He have anything to do with it?"

Such a loaded question. "They're still investigating."

"Well," he said, his gaze on his yard and the field beyond. He sat silent for a long time. Jerry and I waited, not sure what to say. Then Mr. Conrad came back from whatever memory had held him.

"Just thinking about when Nadia's daddy came by and left her with me. I sure as hell didn't know how to look after a baby girl. Didn't want to. But then, I was right glad I did take her in."

"Mr. Conrad, I found a note near the cave," I said. I showed him the picture. "Is this Nadia's handwriting?"

He took the phone for a closer look. "Don't look like it. What's that mean, 'All secrets kept, all debts paid'?"

"That's what I'm trying to find out," I said. "Do you have something with her handwriting on it? When she sent money from Parkland, did she include a letter or a note?"

"Police asked me for all her letters, but there might be one left. Let me go see."

He got up slowly and trudged into his house. He returned in a few minutes and handed me a piece of paper. The letter was written in blue ink on plain stationery:

Dear Papa,

There is more money this time. My new client is very well to do, so I should be able to afford my own place soon. I'd love to have an apartment like Gabrielle's, elegant and overlooking the city. I've had the best time going out to parties there. Some day I'll have a place like this. I'm fine and hope you are too. See you soon!

Love, Nadia

I checked the handwriting with the writing on the note. It was not the same.

I took out my phone. "Do you mind if I take a picture of this letter?"

"Whatever you like. I want justice for my girl."

"We all do, Mr. Conrad," I said.

CHAPTER NINE

We were glad to get back to our house where we could sit on the porch, have sandwiches and big glasses of iced tea, and try to make sense of everything. It was almost seven o'clock, but the sun was still shining brightly. Thanks to the large trees in the front yard and a slight breeze, the porch was shaded and cool.

"Okay," I said. "No sense putting it off." I set my glass of tea beside my rocking chair and dug in my pocket for the plastic bag containing the fiber I'd found near Nadia's body. I compared it with Bill's shirt. "This looks exactly the same."

To make certain, I took the shirt and the fiber out to the front yard and looked at them in a bright patch of sunlight. I came back to the porch and sat holding the shirt despondently for a few minutes before Jerry said, "Maybe someone put fibers under Nadia's fingernails to implicate Bill. I'm sure he's pissed off enough people in his lifetime."

"Yes, but…" I let my voice trail off.

"What about your pal, Milton? He could examine the fiber for you. Find out for certain if it's the same."

I grimaced. Milton Warwick was a scientist who had helped me on previous cases, but I hadn't called on him in quite a while. Even though he knew I was married, he still held out hope I would tire of Jerry and run to his lab, certain his somewhat mantis-like appearance was what I truly dreamed of. "I suppose."

Jerry grinned. "You know Milton would love to see you."

"That sounds like a plan. And what about the mystery note? Assuming that it is related to the murder, if Nadia didn't write it, does that mean her killer did? When he or she wrote 'All debts paid,' did that mean, 'Now you're dead, too'?"

"'Too'? How many people has the Evil Note Writer killed?" Jerry took a drink of his tea. "'All secrets kept, all debts paid.' Sounds like the tag line of a movie."

"You may be on to something." I took out my phone. "Let's see if Google knows." I typed in "All secrets kept, all debts paid," and in a few seconds, the result popped up. "Jerry, you're a genius. It's the tag line for a movie, and not just any old movie." I turned my phone so he could see the poster for *Encounter With Doom*. "A UFO movie."

He leaned over for a better look. "I've never heard of *Encounter With Doom*. What's the date on it?"

I scrolled down. "It's one of those B movies from the Fifties, but it was re-issued in color six years ago. Here's the synopsis. 'Despite their differences, four brave teenagers come together to save Earth from an alien invasion.' Rated eighteen percent on Rotten Tomatoes."

"Four brave teenagers. What do you want to bet this was Nadia's old gang's favorite movie?"

"We need to watch it." I went to YouTube and searched for *Encounter With Doom*. Jerry moved his rocking chair so he could see the screen. The movie was as bad as we expected. The main characters were a snooty rich girl named Princess, a good-looking boy named Ranger, a nerdy boy named Dud, and a pretty girl from the wrong side of town named Fancy. Each one had the Fifties equivalent of a dreadful secret. Princess had a drinking problem, Nerd Boy was a raving marijuana addict, and Ranger and Fancy were fooling around behind Princess's back. Each swore to keep the others' secret, which for some reason was the only way they could defeat the aliens. We never did figure that part out. At the most crucial point in the movie, everything stopped while Ranger took out his guitar and sang in a cringe-worthy attempt to sound like Elvis. The song was Space Babes Are Hot, or something like that, and everybody danced.

In order to keep the low budget low, the aliens were represented by glowing blobs of light that pulsed different colors, green when they were discussing invasion plans with each other, yellow when they were cackling maniacally, and red when those pesky kids interfered with their plans..

"Mood Aliens," Jerry said. "Traffic Light Aliens."

In the end, the aliens were blown up, Earth was saved, and everybody danced again.

"That was so profound," Jerry said. "I want to watch it again."

"This little cinematic treasure would have resonated with Nadia's group," I said. I checked the time. Almost ten. The sky was dark,

"How about a little *Aida*?" Jerry asked.

I stifled a yawn. "Just a little."

Jerry went inside to the parlor which was now his music room and found the aria he wanted to hear.

After listening to several minutes of passionate Italian voices, I asked, "What are they singing about?"

"The high priest, Ramphis, has just told Radames, our hero, that he is the chosen one. 'Mortal, beloved of the gods, to thee is confided the fate of Egypt. Let the holy sword tempered by the gods, in thy hand become to the enemy, terror—a thunderbolt—death.'"

"It's never a good idea to be the Chosen One," I said. "Now Radames has to go around smiting everyone with his thunderbolt sword."

"And singing about it."

I yawned again. "Well, that's enough singing for me."

I thought I was sleepy, but when Jerry and I went upstairs to bed, I couldn't sleep. Besides the problem of Bill and his dark blue shirt with the matching fiber, the idea of Nadia coming to Celosia to visit one of her high school landmarks made no sense. Neither did someone forcing her there, or luring her there. What was the killer's motive? Everyone spoke highly of Nadia, and she certainly had my respect for choosing to resist Bill's offer of an affair.

I rolled over and punched my pillow into shape. Nadia came to town Monday before last to stay a few days with her grandfather. She stopped by Super Food and chatted with her former co-workers on Tuesday. She had lunch with Lon at Deely's on Wednesday. If she was killed on Saturday, that left her whereabouts Thursday and Friday still unaccounted for. Would Coreen Overmeyer be able to fill in the blanks? I certainly hoped so. The only clues I had so far were a dark blue fiber and a quote from a truly awful UFO movie. Despite my previous accomplishments, tonight I did not feel like a successful private investigator. Finally, I pushed back the covers and walked down the hall to my studio.

Previously, the upstairs parlor had been filled with dark, uncomfortable furniture and books, many of them about the care and feeding of bats, Uncle Val's favorite animal and the subject of his studies. Now, thanks to Nell's paint job and improvements, the room was filled with light, my easel, and my art supplies. Completed works and works in progress, plus commissions were stacked against the walls. I took out my mixed emotions on a landscape that rapidly became a modern art collage, smears of dark blue for Bill's shirt and splotches of gold and white for all those UFOs. I added a bit of green for Juniper's cursed alien necklace and a dark patch or two to represent Rodman Fogarty and whatever the hell he might be up to.

After I'd made a fine mess of the landscape, I washed my brushes and my hands and returned to bed. It would have been nice to discover the answer to Nadia's murder in all the swirls of color, but I was going to have to find another way to solve this mystery.

CHAPTER TEN

Wednesday my phone rang at seven thirty. Jerry made a grumpy noise and burrowed further under the covers. He had the morning off from Deely's and intended to sleep late. I stared blearily at the caller ID.

"It's R.W. Jessup," I said in surprise. "What could he be calling about?"

Jerry's voice was muffled. "Maybe the UFO is back."

R.W.'s voice was higher and squeakier than usual. "Madeline, you'll never believe this! There's a genuine crop circle smack dab in the middle of my field! The boys went out to start baling the corn stalks, and there it was. I told 'em not to do anything till you had a look at it. Damndest thing I ever saw. You know where my farm is? Just past the Jenson place 'bout a quarter mile from Old River Road. I told the boys not to tell anyone, but they'd already posted pictures on Facebook, so now I got people everywhere taking pictures. How soon can you get here?"

"I'll be right there." I ended the call and poked the lump that was Jerry. "R.W.'s found a crop circle in his corn field."

Jerry threw back the covers, wide awake. "A crop circle? Neat! Proof positive of alien invaders."

"From what R.W. told me, the whole town's excited. We'd better get there before it's all pulled up for souvenirs."

Jerry was already up and halfway dressed. In about fifteen minutes we were both ready and hopped into the Jeep.

I had no idea where the Jenson place was, but Old River Road was on my GPS, and really, all we had to do was follow the line of cars. Jerry parked the Jeep behind someone's over large pickup truck, and we walked out to the field where crowds of people were taking pictures and videos and selfies, some standing on their cars to get a better view. R.W.'s boys tried to keep folks from wandering into the field, but they weren't having much success. The idea of following the pattern was as thrilling as a Halloween corn maze, and it wasn't until the police arrived that any order was restored.

Chief Brenner spoke through a bullhorn. "All right, everyone, take your pictures and clear out. This is private property, after all, and Mr. Jessup has been patient enough. I'm sure there's an explanation for this, and as soon as we know it, we'll get the word out to you. If anyone knows who is responsible, I'd appreciate you sharing this information."

"Didn't aliens do it?" someone called from the crowd. "There've been circles like this all over the world."

"No one knows for sure," someone else said.

Another voice chimed in. "Probably just kids playing a prank."

"We'll find out," the Chief said. "Now, please move along."

As his officers directed traffic, R.W. approached him, his small features scrunched and bright red.

"If some kids did this, they are going to pay. These stalks were going to feed my cows, and now a big chunk of the field is ruined!"

The Chief switched off the bullhorn. "Did you or your boys see anyone around the field yesterday? Find any footprints or tire tracks that don't belong?"

"No, sir, and I didn't see no dang aliens, neither. If somebody thinks this is funny, I'll have my hungry cows come moo under his window at night and see how funny he thinks that is."

I could tell by Jerry's attempts to keep a straight face that this mental picture was actually pretty entertaining, but he didn't say anything until the Chief asked him a question.

"Jerry, this friend of yours, Rodman Fogarty, the alien expert. Is this something he'd do to drum up interest for his book?"

"It's really not his style."

"That lunatic fella who thinks Carson's Crater's a UFO landing site?" R.W. said. "He'd better not be responsible."

"You can ask him yourself," Jerry said.

We turned to see Rodman Fogarty hop out of his car and stride toward us. "I came as soon as I heard the news! Where is this remarkable phenomenon?"

R.W. glared up at him. "What exactly do you know about it?"

"Crop circles are symbols of complex alien languages that we are only beginning to understand. They could be directions or claims or clan markings. They are amazing mysteries waiting to be unlocked."

"That's not what I meant!"

"Mr. Fogarty," Chief Brenner said, "did you have anything to do with the creation of this crop circle?"

He drew back, one hand to his chest. "Me? Certainly not! How could I have possibly made it?"

"Well, someone did, and if you have any information, you'd be wise to tell me."

"Of course!" he said. "I always cooperate fully with law enforcement. Now, may I please have a closer look?"

Chief Brenner glanced at R.W. The little farmer sighed, exasperated. "Take your pictures and go," he said, "and I'd better not catch you back here again."

Fogarty already had his phone out and headed for the field.

"R.W., I'd like to have a look around," I said. "I might be able to find out what caused this circle."

"You go right ahead," he said.

The Chief agreed, so Jerry and I followed Fogarty.

"I'll go this way," Jerry said, veering off towards R.W.'s boys.

I caught up with Fogarty. "Mind if I tag along? I think this is fascinating."

"I'd be delighted to have your company," he said. "I am so fortunate to be here at the time of such a remarkable occurrence. I can only believe the aliens who landed here years ago, the very aliens I talk about in *True Invasion*, are returning."

One of them is already here, I thought, noting the fanatical gleam in his eyes.

"Would there be any other explanations for a crop circle?" I asked.

"Scientists will try to tell you it's the weather, whirlwinds, mini-tornadoes and the like, but I am a certified cereologist. I know what I'm seeing."

"A cereologist?"

"Someone who studies crop circles. Named after Ceres, the Roman goddess of agriculture. Look at this pattern! The wind can't do this."

The corn had been harvested and the stalks left for baling, except for the ones that had been bent down to the ground into a pattern of interlocking circles with an odd key-shaped formation at one end. Could someone have trampled the stalks into these circles? It would take a lot of trampling, or many people working together to march around. Or maybe they used some sort of farm machinery? But wouldn't there be tracks and footprints? They'd have to get into the field somehow, and I didn't see any tracks or footprints. Although R. W. was incensed that a "big chunk" of his field had been ruined, I could see that the stalks weren't ruined, merely flattened and could probably be salvaged.

The corn field was bordered on one long side by a wheat field and the driveway to R.W.'s farm house on another. The front of the field met the road, and the back was fenced in to keep the cows wandering in the pasture beyond from getting into the corn. Aside from the trampled grass where eager Celosians had gathered to take pictures and gawk, I couldn't see any signs of entry. Could someone have parachuted into the field? That would be a long way to go for a prank.

Fogarty continued to rhapsodize and take pictures. "This is perfect for my next book. I could call it *Circling Back to Earth*—no, wait. *Alien Crop*. No, that sounds too choppy. Maybe *Alien Harvest*. Yes, I like that."

I hated to interrupt his creative flow, but it was facts I wanted. "What about something underneath the field causing the circles?"

"Underneath? Oh, you mean the earth's magnetic field? Highly unlikely."

"But iron filings swirl around the ends of a magnet."

"That theory has been raised and disproven many times, Madeline. This is a real alien crop circle and must be preserved and studied."

"But is it possible someone could have made it?"

"Well, back in the Seventies, there were some pranksters in Britain who walked around with a flat board held up by reins, but their circles were obviously inferior and dismissed by true 'croppies.' This one is splendid and could only have been made by aliens." The roar of farm machinery made him whirl around. "What? They can't possibly be thinking of destroying this circle!"

But that was exactly what R.W.'s sons planned to do. Fogarty pushed his way through the field and stopped in front of the machine, hands out. "Stop! What do you think you're doing?"

The husky young man driving the baler put on the brake and yelled over the roar of the engine, "What does it look like I'm doing? Get out of the way."

"You can't do this! This is a vital part of UFO history!"

"It's our field," the young man bellowed. "Back off!"

"You're destroying important evidence!"

"I'm doing my job. Get him out of here, Madeline."

I tugged on Fogarty's arm. "We'll ask Chief Brenner if he agreed to this."

"The police, yes, of course!" Fogarty ran back towards the Chief 's squad car, where Brenner and R.W. stood watching the proceedings. "I must protest this action!"

"Did you get your pictures?" the Chief asked.

"Yes, but certain authorities must be contacted, the media, the world! This is monumental!"

"This is Mr. Jessup's farm. It's private property."

"But you're destroying evidence of alien contact!"

"My people have finished looking around. You've finished looking around. I think we can all move on."

Fogarty spluttered and fussed, but Chief Brenner merely folded his arms and looked at him. Fogarty was tall, but the Chief was an imposing six five, and his calm stare had even unnerved Jerry on occasion. Sensing he'd get no sympathy from either Brenner or the still glaring R.W., Fogarty abruptly turned and stalked away.

"You see anything?" the Chief asked me.

"No, and Fogarty shot down all the popular theories."

"Well, my theory is kids with too much time on their hands. I'm going to talk to some of my more inventive town troublemakers. Let me know if you come up with anything else."

"I will," I said. "Have you got any leads about Nadia?"

"Unfortunately, no."

I located Jerry at the far end of the maze. "Any luck?" I asked.

"Nope. It's impressive, though, isn't it?"

We walked back to where Chief Brenner was finishing a phone call. He put his phone away and pushed back his cap.

"Well, my main culprits are doing community service at the recycling center and the food pantry. The others said they didn't know what a crop circle was or how they were supposed to look. So I'm back to Rodman Fogarty. It's quite a coincidence to have a crop circle suddenly appear when he's in town talking up his UFO book."

The Chief turned to Jerry. "You know this guy, Jerry. Is he a good actor? Because it sure looked like an act to me."

"He's always been a bit over the top," Jerry said, "but I'll talk to him. I may be able to find out."

The chief's phone beeped with a message, and he excused himself to take the call.

"Do you think Fogarty's capable of making a crop circle?" I asked Jerry as we walked back to the Jeep. "He'd need help, wouldn't he? He mentioned something about a hoax in England back in the Seventies."

"He's always been all talk and very little action," Jerry said. "People remember him because he's so annoying. That doesn't work for a con. You have to be as anonymous as possible."

"Could he have hired some other con men to assist him?"

"I suppose he could."

"Can you find out without making him suspicious?"

"Sure."

"Well, I need coffee," I said. "We ran out without any breakfast."

"I can take care of that," he said.

"But it's your day off," I said. "I'll make breakfast."

Jerry was a little skeptical of my cooking skills, but I managed not to burn the toast, and it's almost impossible to ruin milk and cereal. I'd had two cups of coffee and was just about feeling human when the phone rang.

"Good morning, Madeline," came Tucker's cheerful voice. "I'm on my way to Celosia for the Garden Club meeting. I got an early start and thought I'd come pick you up at your house."

I'd almost forgotten the Garden Club meeting. That was today at ten o'clock. My watch said quarter to nine. "Great," I said. "Jerry and I are having breakfast, so come on down," I said.

By the time Tucker's green Subaru Outback came up the drive I'd exchanged my shorts and tee shirt for a white sundress and sandals, a quick application of light pink lipstick, and my best gold earrings.

When I greeted Tucker on the porch, the brothers complimented my fashion choice, and Tucker commented on the lack of flowers in the yard. "Although the wild flowers look nice," he said, "and I see you have plenty of sunflowers. No roses, though. I'll have to take care of that."

"Speaking of roses," I said, "what's the best way to approach Coreen?"

"Flattery, and lots of it." He turned to Jerry. "You're not coming?" Jerry gave him a look that made him laugh. "I didn't think so. We can take my car, Madeline."

***

On the way to Coreen's, I filled Tucker in on my case.

"I need to find a sample of Coreen's handwriting," I said, "so during the meeting, if I slip away, just keep talking."

At the Silver Lakes mansion, we rang the doorbell, and Coreen opened the huge glass door.

"Tucker Fairweather, so nice to see you," she said. "And you must be Madeline Maclin. I got your message. Such a shame about Nadia, isn't it? I'm Coreen Overmeyer. Come in, come in."

Unlike her classmate Nadia, Coreen obviously had every advantage of birth and fortune. She was tall, blond, and tan with distractingly long fake fingernails. She wore a white blouse, a short pink skirt, and fancy jeweled sandals.

She led us through a wide foyer to a sun room at the back of the house where the Celosia Garden Club members had gathered. The sun room stretched the entire back of the house and looked out on a massive garden ablaze with early fall color, including purple and bronze chrysanthemums and masses of red, orange, white, and yellow roses. The meeting area for the Garden Club took up only a quarter of the space, round glass tables with centerpieces of roses and gold and white dishes arranged as for a royal banquet. Most people had chosen their seats, although a few lingered at the windows, admiring the garden. Everyone turned their attention to Coreen.

"Everyone, you know Tucker Fairweather, don't you?" she

said. "He lives in that gorgeous yellow mansion in Parkland and has the most fabulous garden. You've grown a new rose, haven't you, Tucker? You'll have to tell us all about it. And this is Madeline Maclin. I imagine some of you know her, too." She indicated a table near the front. "Tucker, I have a place for you at the main table. There will be a brief business meeting and then we'll want to hear about your new rose. Madeline, you're welcome to sit where you like."

I decided to take a seat at the back. Minutes were read and approved. A motion to plant flowers at the corner of Main and Summer Street was carried. There was a brief debate over the number of canes on bare-root roses. Tucker explained that three or more was the best. Old business was discussed and tabled. New business included using either red or purple striped petunias for SkinkFest. Then Coreen introduced Tucker again, and he stood to tell about his success in cultivating Lillian.

All of the attention was on Tucker. I asked the ladies at my table where to find the restroom and was directed to the hallway. I quietly got out of my seat and left the sunroom. I entered the foyer. A quick glance showed me the rooms off the foyer were a parlor, a dining room, and another seating area, all devoid of writing materials. I knew Tucker could talk about roses for hours, so I decided to take a chance and go upstairs.

Besides guest rooms, there was a master bedroom that commanded a sweeping view of the back gardens. The en suite was as big as my bedroom, and my living room would have easily fit into the walk in closet. In all the rooms, everything was beige and cream, from the silky draperies to the array of fancy little pillows artfully arranged on the matching bedspreads. Crystal chandeliers dangled from each ceiling. There were paintings, vases, ornate clocks, and thick rugs with swirly patterns. However, there was a sad lack of any writing. No books, no magazines, no diary on the bedside table, no postcard stuck in the gold frame of the mirror.

Well, I thought, how often do I write a letter? I always text. Occasionally, I sent a birthday or Christmas card. I should have realized that Coreen's generation rarely had to write anything. Even a grocery list could be on the cell phone.

I had noticed a group of framed photographs on the dresser in one of the guest bedrooms. A quick glance showed me the pictures were mainly of Coreen in various poses. Coreen at the beach. Coreen at the Eiffel Tower. Coreen on the deck of what must be her yacht. But on closer inspection, I saw the smallest picture was of the four high school friends. Coreen affected a model pose, pouty and slightly bored. Nadia looked the same as the picture Bill had shown me, her dark bangs tangled by the wind, her smile bright. The fellow with the shaggy hair, glasses, and a goofy grin was Lon. He'd definitely improved with age. And I recognized the other young man from his picture in the Celosia News. Patrick Thompson.

A nice picture and not unusual for four good friends to stop for a photo op. What was unusual was the spot they'd chosen. If I wasn't mistaken, they were standing at the entrance to Carson's Cave. Down in one corner of the picture was a date written in tiny numbers. September 17, the date of Patrick Thompson's death.

So they'd all been there when his "accident" happened.

I took a picture of this photograph and made my way back downstairs to the foyer. My timing was perfect. Tucker had finished answering questions and sat down as the group applauded.

I slid back into my seat and joined in the applause.

Coreen stood, encouraged more applause, and then said,

"Thank you so much, Tucker. That was wonderful. Everyone, brunch is on the way, and after that, I'll be giving tours of my garden." She indicated a table filled with plates of fancy crackers and cheese and a variety of fruit on sticks positioned along the side of the room. "For now, please enjoy the hors d'oeuvres."

I made my way to the table and took a few of the fruit skewers. Coreen kept talking to Tucker, but I caught his eye and he politely excused himself to move to another group of interested rose fans. As Coreen turned, seeking more admirers, I angled myself in her path.

"Everything is absolutely beautiful," I said. "I can't wait to see your garden,"

"It is a showplace, I must admit," she said. "Do you have a garden?"

"A small one. Tucker's going to help me get it into shape."

She gave me a condescending smile. "Well, sometimes you have to start small. I'd be happy to give you some advice."

"That would be very nice of you," I said, "but I was hoping you could give me some information that might shed some light on Nadia Conrad's murder."

Her smile faded. "I doubt that."

"When did you last see Nadia?" I asked. "Kathy Holly told me she might have stayed with you last week."

At the mention of Kathy's name, Coreen huffed in disgust. "Kathy Holly! Still trying to weasel her way in. My God, that was seven years ago. She was not a member of our group, I don't care what she says. Always tagging along. Such a nuisance."

"So you didn't see Nadia?"

"She came by Thursday. She didn't stay long."

"Did she tell you about her life in Parkland?" I asked.

"Just the usual. Looking after some rich man's kids. Sounded boring to me, but then, her life has always sounded boring to me."

"But her murder must have upset you."

Coreen's controlled expression never wavered. "Yes, of course, and I hope you find whoever killed her, but just because we were friends in high school doesn't mean we were friends forever. We had very little in common."

The happy faces I'd seen in the photograph of the four friends at Carson's Cave suggested otherwise.

"Last Saturday was September 17," I said. "Any significance to that date?"

She shrugged. "Not to me."

"Patrick Thompson died on September 17."

"I don't see how that is in any way significant."

"But you were there, weren't you?" I asked, watching her carefully. "That day at the cave? You and Nadia and Lon."

She frowned at me, and spoke in a defensive tone. "What does that have to do with anything? Why are you interested in something that happened years ago?" A man in a white shirt and black slacks motioned to her from the doorway, and she said, "Oh, that's the caterer," unmistakably relieved. "Excuse me, please. I'd better make sure he brought everything I paid for."

Tucker made his way through his fans to me. "Any luck?" he asked.

"Not a scrap of writing anywhere," I said. "I'll have to figure out another way."

"Coreen probably has people to write for her," he said.

A bell rang, and Coreen announced that brunch was served. Tucker went back to his seat.

Fortunately for the caterer, Coreen's order was correct. We enjoyed little flower-shaped chicken sandwiches, fruit in tall glasses, fancy smelly cheese, and petit fours decorated with candied pansies. Coreen worked the room, checking in with each table to make sure everyone had enough to eat and drink and accepting compliments on her garden.

When she returned to our table, I asked her to point out her Prestige rose. Before I followed her, I dug a pen out of my pocketbook along with a scrap of paper from an old receipt.

She led me to the sun room window. "Right there, the pink and white one in the middle."

The rose was a beautiful pink color trimmed in white. "It's lovely," I said.

"As it grows, it becomes more white and the pink is the trim," she said. "A reversal of the colors."

"That must have taken you quite a while to create."

"Totally worth it. My husband said he didn't care how much money it took. He supported me one hundred percent. It's won all sorts of prizes, and been featured in *Rose Growers Monthly*, *New Rose Digest*, and several other prominent gardening magazines."

Roses of the Rich and Famous. I handed her the piece of paper and the pen. "Would you write those titles down for me? I'd love to read the articles about Prestige."

"Oh, I'll text them to you."

Strike Two. I looked back at the sunroom and the people visiting in little groups or chatting at their tables and decided to give my investigation one more try. "Would you mind answering a few more questions about Nadia?"

She gave me a hard stare. "Yes, I would." She checked her diamond wrist watch. "All right, everyone. Who wants a tour of my garden?"

CHAPTER ELEVEN

A fter Coreen's tour, Tucker escorted me back to his car. He was beaming.

I thought I knew why. "Nice to have all that admiration for Lillian, isn't it?"

"Oh, it's better than that," he said. "Hop in."

Intrigued, I got in the car. Tucker presented me with a flower catalog.

"Okay," I said. "This is nice, but you know I have limited garden experience."

"Open it."

I turned the page. On the back of the cover page was a written message that said, "Dear Tucker, thank you so much for gracing us with your expertise and for your many wonderful compliments on Prestige. Coreen Overmeyer."

I looked up into his gray eyes—so much like Jerry's—and had to laugh. "You sneaky rascal."

"I asked her for her autograph. Told you all it took was lots and lots of flattery."

I pulled out my phone and compared the writing with the note. My elation faded.

"They don't match, do they?" Tucker said,

"No, but at least I can eliminate Coreen as the Evil Note Writer. Good work, partner."

He started the car and drove down the street toward home. "So who does that leave?"

"Of the four friends, Lon Forest."

"Have you talked to him?"

"Yes, but there wasn't a chance to get a sample of his handwriting. He seems very upset about Nadia's death, though, whereas Coreen dismissed their friendship and refused to answer any more questions. But either of these reactions could be misleading."

We passed a few more overlarge houses before turning out of Coreen's neighborhood. Tucker gave me a brief glance. "Are all your cases this complicated?"

"Pretty much. The folks who grew up in Celosia are a tight knit bunch, and they all went to the one high school in town, and they all know each other's business. This can be helpful, but only if they want to talk. I'm still considered an outsider and a nosy one at that."

"But you've solved several murders. That's got to count for something."

"You'd think so, but usually I uncover things that people think should stay hidden." And I was beginning to believe Patrick Thompson's accident was one of those things.

***

Tucker wanted to see what Jerry and I had done inside the Eberlin House lately, so when we got home, I gave him the tour. We wandered from the living room—light blue instead of gray and now cobweb-free—to the upstairs rooms, including my studio, where he admired my latest portraits and the Frustration Collage.

"Looks like a lot of emotion went into that one," he said.

"Some days it's either paint or pop."

We went back downstairs where he peeked into the parlor. The large dining room table and set of eight chairs had been moved out to make room for a couple of armchairs and Jerry's old brown upright piano. "I see this is the music room."

"Better than the séance room."

He chuckled. "Is he still doing that?"

"No, thank goodness."

"Don't tell me he's completely reformed."

I wasn't sure how much Tucker knew about his brother's shady background. "He's working on it." Another thought occurred to me. "You know him as well as anyone. When you were growing up, did he ever mention something he wanted to do? I can't imagine his life's goal was to hold phony séances and play games with other peoples' money."

Tucker sat down at the piano and played a few chords. "Well, we all wanted to be musicians, but Des got all the talent there. Then I discovered my love of gardening, and when the house was left to me, I suddenly had all the garden I could ever wish for. Jerry was always off somewhere. I never actually heard him say, 'Oh, I want to be an explorer in the Amazon,' or 'Gee, archeology looks like fun.' Nothing specific. He just loved having adventures. Kinda makes me surprised he settled down in a small town like Celosia."

"Oh, we have plenty of adventures here," I said.

He thanked me for the tour and said he ought to get home. "There's always something that needs watering."

I told him to tell Selene hello from me. "Bring her along next time."

"If I can get her out of the garden," he said. His wife loved flowers even more than he did.

It was past one o'clock, but I'd had enough to eat at Coreen's brunch. Jerry hadn't called or sent a text, and I wondered if he was still with Fogarty. The man seemed genuinely excited about the crop circle and upset when it was destroyed, but then again, he was a con man, despite his declaration all that was behind him. I'd seen how easily Jerry could modify his emotions depending on circumstances. He was quite skilled at manipulating people. I liked to think I could see through all his tricks.

I took a glass of tea out to the porch, planning to text Jerry and see when he'd be home, when to my surprise, Bill called.

"Madeline, have you found out who killed Nadia yet? Have you found out anything at all?"

I took a big drink of tea. Bill was in combat mode and I needed to fortify myself for battle. "I would like to ask you about Gabrielle Grey."

"What about her?"

"Well, you neglected to mention her before."

"What's that got to do with anything? Is Gabrielle a suspect?"

He sounded eager to shift the blame to someone else.

"I'm following every lead I can find, Bill. I don't get results overnight," I said. "What other friends did Nadia have in Parkland?"

"I have no idea. She came here, looked after the kids, and then she went home to that little apartment of hers. And don't ask if I ever went there because I didn't."

Well, according to Chief Brenner, Nadia's neighbors had seen him there and heard him assuring Nadia she needn't worry about money.

Was he always this bull-headed? How in the world did I ever love him in the first place? I must have been desperate to get married. That had to be the answer. Desperate to be married and no longer eligible for Miss America. Although there was always Mrs. America.

This ridiculous and possibly true answer surprised a laugh from me that made Bill even angrier.

"I fail to see any humor in this situation, Madeline! You're not the one who's a person of interest in Nadia's murder."

He sounded defeated. I managed to find some compassion. "Bill, I'm truly sorry it's come to this. Did you talk to Tina?"

"Tina took the girls to visit their grandmother for a while. The atmosphere in the house isn't the best right now. Of course, I can't leave town until this is settled, and the police have talked to me for hours. Practically all one day, and then they had me come in for another half day of questions."

"I assure you I'm doing all I can."

There was a long pause. I wondered if he was going to hang up again. But when he spoke, his tone had changed. "Madeline," he said. "I'm sorry. I've been a jerk. I know you're trying to help me, and I appreciate it."

Well, this was new. "Just continue to cooperate with the police," I said. "We'll figure this out."

"'All right," he said. "Thank you."

He ended the call. I sat staring at my phone for a few minutes. I guess it took something as serious as a murder accusation to make Bill say thank you.

I was starting to get concerned about Jerry when he called. "I'm on my way home," he said. "You still want to take the fiber to

Warwick?"

"Yes," I said. "I need proof positive that it did or did not come from Bill's shirt."

When Jerry got to the house, we decided to take my car to Milton Warwick's home in Parkland. He hopped into the passenger's seat. "I can tell by the gleam in your eyes you've already had a full day."

"You will be proud to know Tucker succeeded in getting a sample of Coreen's handwriting."

"Always knew he had it in him."

"It didn't match the note," I said. "But I did see a photo of the four friends, and they were standing at the entrance to Carson's Cave."

"Would this have been the day of Patrick's accident?"

"Yes, September 17. And no one's arm was stretched out to take the picture, so it wasn't a selfie. I wonder who took the picture."

"Maybe they had a tripod and a timer."

"Maybe. And I had another conversation with Bill, who, believe it or not, thanked me for staying on the case."

"What?" Jerry said in mock surprise. "I'm glad I'm not driving, or I would've run off the road."

I drove down Main Street so we could admire all the Skinkfest trimmings, striped flags, striped banners, and large cutouts of skinks dressed like farmers, ballerinas, and clowns with holes for people to stick their heads through for a Skink photo op.

"Looks like everyone's about ready for Friday," Jerry said.

"Did you learn anything from Fogarty?" I asked.

"The entire history of crop circles in North America. Did you know a mysterious circle of fried soy beans was discovered in Iowa in 1969? And a burned circle in Connecticut in 1970 that a woman said was caused by a spaceship landing in the grass?"

"Sounds fascinating," I said, "but not very helpful."

"He's still highly annoyed that R.W.'s son baled up the one in the Jessup's field. I think he saw it as his premiere discovery."

"Any hint that he might have made it himself?"

"I steered the conversation in that direction by asking him if he thought it could've been a local hoax. He said, and I quote, 'There is no one in this rustic little berg with the skill or imagination, especially not those Neanderthal farm boys.'"

"I hope they don't ever catch him saying that."

"When I told him he could show them how it's done, he said he was above that sort of prank. I asked if he kept in touch with any of the old gang, and he said no because proving the existence of aliens was his primary focus. But something's bugging him, and I don't think it's the ruined crop circle."

I turned off Main onto the road that led to Parkland. "So you think he's a threat?"

"If he is, he's doing a damn fine job of hiding it."

CHAPTER TWELVE

Milton Warwick lived in a narrow little house in a neighborhood of narrow little houses spaced evenly along a short street, each with its own little strip of front yard. I parked out front and reached into the back seat for Bill's shirt. I heaved a sigh.

"Here we go."

Jerry's eyes were alight with mischief. "I am looking forward to Milton's reaction."

Warwick answered the door, and his eyes lit up, too, but with delight, a delight that dimmed as he realized Jerry was with me.

"Madeline! Jerry! Welcome!" He pressed his spindly form against the door so we could enter. "Come in. To what do I owe the honor of this visit?"

"I hope we're not interrupting an experiment," I said. Warwick's house, as far as I could see, consisted of small living quarters, a lab, and this front room, which resembled a dentist's waiting room.

"Oh, no, no. Have a seat, please."

There were three white plastic chairs and a matching table with magazines and a lamp with a dingy shade. The magazines were copies of *Astounding Nonsense*, a publication of the Parkland Science Club, a magazine devoted to discussions of bizarre discoveries and inventions.

Jerry and I sat down, and Warwick folded himself into the third chair. He looked the same as always, tall and thin, with a domed head and long fingers. "I hope all is well in Celosia," he said. "I follow your adventures on YouTube, Madeline. Quite a lot going on in that little town of yours."

"More than I ever thought there would be," I said. "I'm investigating the murder of a young woman, and I have some things that require your expertise."

"Delighted to be of service."

I handed him Bill's shirt. "I have a fiber that might match this shirt," I said. I pulled the baggie containing the fiber from my pocket.

"No problem! Come with me."

The last time I'd asked for Warwick's help, I'd stayed in the waiting room while he checked out the authenticity of a dollar bill. This time, both Jerry and I were invited into the laboratory.

I expected something along the lines of Frankenstein's lab, but Warwick's was spotlessly clean and white. He motioned us to the counter and a gleaming microscope.

"Shouldn't take but a minute," he said. He placed the fiber on a slide and adjusted the microscope. He peered at the fiber. "Mm, hmm. Got it. Now the shirt." He arranged the shirt so that a small portion was under the microscope. After a few tense moments, he said. "Yep. It matches."

I felt all the air go out of my body. Jerry put his arm around my shoulders. "Still doesn't mean he did it," he said.

Warwick pulled the shirt free and started to hand it back.

"Dear me. Are you all right?"

I managed to get my breath. "That shirt belongs to my ex-husband."

"Oh," he said. "Oh. I see. But this is an extremely popular brand of shirt, Madeline. There must be hundreds of thousands of them. You must keep that in mind."

Right now, I wanted to think about anything else. "Thank you."

"Anything for you," he said gallantly. "I sincerely hope your ex-husband is innocent."

"That's what I hope to prove," I said.

But it didn't look good.

***

As soon as we got into the car, I said, "Damn it."

"Okay, maybe enough investigating for today," Jerry said. "You need a fun activity. Do you want to look for a striped dress for SkinkFest while we're in town?"

"No, I'll get one in Celosia," I said. "I like to shop local when I can, and since SkinkFest is fast approaching, there should be lots of striped stuff to choose from. I hope you have a striped tie to wear."

"I can do one better than that. I have a tie with lizards on it."

Jerry's tie collection took up an entire section of his closet. "I believe you have two ties with lizards on them," I said. "How will you choose?"

"It will be a difficult decision." He gave me a searching look. "You're sure you're okay?"

Was I okay? I wasn't sure.

"Well," I said, "I just have to keep reminding myself there are thousands of dark blue shirts in the world."

"That's true. And it's highly doubtful Bill knows about Carson's Cave."

My phone dinged with a text message and I asked Jerry to see who it was.

"You might want to pull over and answer this one," he said. "It's your mom."

I turned into the nearest gas station and parked at the far end and read my mother's message.

"Michael and I are married!" it began with a highly unusual exclamation mark.

"We had the loveliest little ceremony at a divine chateau in the countryside just outside of Paris. Michael rented it for the whole weekend. He even arranged for a string quartet to play for the service and had fireworks over the lake afterwards. We're on our way to our honeymoon in Monaco. I wish you could have been here, but I'm sending pictures."

My phone chimed, signaling the arrival of wedding photos. I scrolled through the pictures. Mom looked slim and elegant as always in a cream-colored dress with just a hint of lace. She stood arm in arm with Big Mike, who wore a formal black tux with a grey silk tie. Both of them were beaming. More pictures showed them posed on the patio of the chateau overlooking the vineyards, standing beside a willow tree in a lush garden, sitting by an ornate fish pond filled with koi and water lilies, and raising glasses of champagne with a small group of guests.

"These are beautiful," I texted back. "Congratulations! I love you."

After a few minutes, she replied with the heart emoji.

A heart emoji. From my mother. This was so unexpected and so wonderfully out of character, I sat and smiled at the heart for several minutes before passing my phone to Jerry.

He looked through the pictures and then gave me a hopeful look. "So what do you think about that?"

I found I could answer with complete honesty. "I'm really happy for both of them."

***

Our trip to Parkland hadn't taken as long as I expected, so we were back home around four. I decided I wasn't finished with investigating for the day. As luck would have it, a call from Loraine Forest gave me the perfect opportunity to visit.

"Madeline, I hate to bother you," she said, "but Roger is missing and Lonny's at school. I can't see well enough to look for him, and if he's hurt, I don't know if I'd hear him crying. Could you possibly spare a few minutes to come look for him?"

"I'll be right there," I said. "Case of the Missing Cat," I told Jerry. "A good chance to get a sample of Lon's handwriting."

"Need backup?"

"I think I can handle it," I said.

***

I had to speak loudly for Loraine to hear. "Where did you last see Roger?"

She waved her hand vaguely around her porch. "Oh, here and there. He's so dark, it's hard for me to see him sometimes."

"Have you looked inside?"

"Everywhere I could think of."

"Let's look again," I said. Roger could be curled up underneath a chair where Loraine couldn't see or even bend down to look.

"Oh, Roger's favorite place to sleep is on Lonny's bed. Sheds all over the comforter, but Lonny says he doesn't mind." She led the way down the hall and pushed open the door. A king-sized bed dominated the small room, and on the bed was Roger. He'd made himself a nest of clothes. He looked up at us as if to say, "Yes? Did you want something?"

"Roger, you naughty boy," Loraine said. "I looked in here for you. Where were you hiding?"

Roger yawned and rolled over.

Loraine peered closer at the pile of shirts. "I wish to goodness Lonny would pick up his dirty clothes. Now they'll have cat hair all over them."

One of Lon's shirts was dark blue.

"Let me get those for you," I said.

"Oh, now, you don't have to do that," she said.

"It's no trouble." Besides tee shirts featuring comic book characters and logos for movies and TV shows, there were two dark blue shirts, exactly the same brand and style as Bill's, but they looked new. I gave them a close inspection before folding them up with the others. "Where would you like these?"

"What?"

"Where would you like these? Do you have a laundry room?"

"No, no, you leave them right there. I'll take care of them."

I asked Loraine when Lon would be home from school. I had to repeat my question two more times before she understood.

"You know, I'm not sure about his schedule," she said. "He comes and goes."

"What's his phone number?"

"Oh, I do know that." She told me Lon's number, and I put it in my phone.

I took another look around Lon's bedroom, hoping to find something with his handwriting on it. A small bookshelf was crammed with paperback books, mostly science fiction novels. On the night stand a lamp shared space with a bag of potato chips and an empty soda can. No journal or notebook. No textbooks, either, but he could have taken those to his classes. A flat screen TV took up the top of the bureau, a stack of DVDs next to it. I expected one of the DVDs to be *Encounter With Doom*, but there wasn't a copy of the clique's favorite movie in the stack. There were a couple of coasters, though, from "Betty's Bingo Bar."

"My goodness," Loraine said. "Looks like Lonny's bought himself some new shoes." She indicated three shoeboxes stacked by the night stand. "His other sneakers must have worn out."

"Do you mind if I have a look?" I asked. The shoes were very expensive name brand sneakers. "Wow, these are nice. I'll have to tell Jerry to get some."

"I think Lonny orders online," she said. "The mail carrier is always delivering packages."

I asked Loraine if there was anything else I could do for her before I left.

"That's very sweet of you, Madeline," she said. "I'm fine, thank you."

I drove back to my office and made a few calls. A call to Parkland Community College connected me with a secretary who told me the schedule for the science classes. None of those classes met that day. Even more interesting, there was no one named Lon Forest enrolled at PCC.

My next call was to Lon's number. It went to a full message box.

I sat back in my chair. Obviously, Lon had been lying to his mother, living in the house rent free, and taking money off the kitchen table to spend on new sneakers but not new hearing aids.

CHAPTER THIRTEEN

Jerry had made my favorite chicken and rice for supper, and after a generous helping and a large glass of tea, I discussed what I'd discovered in Lon's bedroom.

"Three pairs of high-end sneakers?" he said. "Loraine must have more money than I thought."

"And I don't think Lon can make very much cash playing Bingo."

"What makes you say that?"

"Just something Loraine mentioned," I said. "He's supposed to take his mother to Betty's Bingo Bar, but I doubt he ever does. He's got some coasters from the place, though."

Jerry began to laugh. "Betty's is an illegal casino."

"What?"

"There are only four legal casinos in the state, and they aren't anywhere near here, so Betty's Bingo Bar has become inventive. Bingo in the front, casino in the back."

"Can you just walk in?"

"No, but I remember the password."

Of course he remembered the password. "Well, Lon isn't at Parkland Community College and never has been," I said. "Why don't we drive over to Betty's?"

Jerry was ready for the hunt. We took his Jeep and drove to the outskirts of Celosia into a seedy little neighborhood called Dry Bridge. Dry Bridge was beyond dry. It consisted of a dead and empty car dealership, two tumbledown storage buildings, and a larger flat topped building that might have been a grocery store in its youth attached to a gas station with a faded red and yellow sign that read "Betty's Bingo Bar." The beige Oldsmobile was parked on the far side of the lot. Closer inspection revealed it had a dented back bumper.

"That's the right car," I said.

Jerry backed the Jeep into a parking space on the back row where we had a view of the entrance to the bingo hall. "What do you want to do?"

"I know Lon comes to Deely's, or he did when he met Nadia for lunch last Wednesday." I asked. "Does he know you?"

"We've never met."

"Then I'm sending you in," I said. "He's a tall dark man, twenty-five, stubble, dark eyes, and a sharp little nose, most likely wearing either a dark blue shirt or a tee shirt with a pop culture logo. If you can, find out where he was last Saturday night. Oh, and see if you can get a sample of his handwriting."

"Got it."

I could tell by the gleam in his eyes he couldn't wait. He hopped out of the Jeep. He paused to grin and ask a question. "How much money do you want me to win?"

I ignored this. "Text me if there's trouble."

"No trouble."

As I watched him enter the bingo hall, I felt a rising sense of anxiety. Lon Forest didn't know Jerry, but there could be people inside who did, people angling for Big Mike's job who wanted to know where he was and might not be polite about it. But if I went in, Lon would recognize me. I'd just have to trust Jerry's skill at evading difficult situations.

Depending on the type of game Jerry was going to play, I wasn't sure how long I'd have to wait, but after an hour and a half he hurried back to the Jeep and jumped in. He handed me a wad of bills.

"Jerry."

"I couldn't help it," he said. "We can give it to the Orphan Skinks Home. Besides, I needed to see if Lon's a sore loser. And he is." He started the Jeep. "We should go."

"Did you make him that mad?"

"Yep." He drove the Jeep around the corner, pulled in behind a delivery van, and cut the engine. "The Oldsmobile should be screeching by very soon."

"Tell me what happened."

"He was easy to spot. I asked some of the regulars if he was in last Saturday. They said no, and one guy said that was unusual because Lon came in most nights and played until past closing. 'Would you say he has a problem?' I asked, and he laughed and said, 'Everybody in here does.' I got into a poker game with him and a few other folks. I bought several rounds of drinks. Chatted about work. He said that was for other people, not him. Changed the subject to women. He said they were all alike, cheaters, heart breakers. I told him a long story about a girl I'd known since we were in high school, and I thought we had a future, but she left me. 'I hear you,' he said. Since the mystery note we found mentioned a secret, I said, 'Well, she had some kind of secret she'd never tell me.'"

I recalled my conversation with Lon in his mother's rose garden. "Any reaction?"

"He took a big swig of his drink and said, 'Women can't keep secrets.' By then, he was not winning and not happy about it," Jerry said. "Got quite a temper. He wanted a rematch, but I said I had to go, and that's when he blew up. Oh, here he comes now. Duck."

We ducked down as the beige Oldsmobile careened around the corner and flew past. I managed to catch a glimpse of Lon's face, dark with anger.

We sat up, and Jerry started the Jeep. "Do you want to follow him?"

"Yes," I said. "I imagine he's heading home for more money, and I'd like to make sure he's calmed down by then."

We pulled out of the parking lot and drove back toward town. "I didn't get his handwriting, sorry," Jerry said. "I thought about making him write me an I.O.U., but he'd already Hulked out. He was wearing an Incredible Hulk tee shirt, by the way. That tells you something right there."

"Mild-mannered man has burst of wild uncontrollable strength? I can see where Lon would relate."

We followed the Oldsmobile back to Heritage Lane. Jerry parked a safe distance back, and I hopped out of the Jeep for a better view. Lon got out of his car and slammed the door. I watched as he took some deep breaths, straightened his tee shirt, and brushed back his hair. Then he walked calmly up to the porch and opened the screen door, shutting it carefully behind him. I envisioned him bringing up a pleasant smile and a greeting for his mother.

I slid back into the Jeep's passenger seat. "I believe the storm has passed," I said.

"He's not going to do anything to the Bank of Mom," Jerry said.

We waited for about fifteen minutes, and then Lon returned to the Oldsmobile. We followed him just long enough to see him drive back into the parking lot at Betty's Bingo Bar.

"I think Mr. Forest has a problem," Jerry said.

"What does Lon need money for?" I asked as we drove home. "Besides fancy sneakers, that is. He doesn't wear expensive clothes, and he seems content to drive the Oldsmobile. He's already got a big TV. Unless—could he be using his gambling wins to buy drugs? I didn't see any indication of drugs in his room, but that's something he would definitely hide from his mother."

"That's possible," Jerry said, "but gambling can't be a dependable source of income because gambling is a loss. Like tonight. There's always someone who shows up who's a better player, and you have to run back home for more cash. You can never count on winning, but someone who's addicted to gambling will always try one more time. One more roll of the dice, one more pull of the one-armed bandit slot machine. And Lon doesn't strike me as a drug addict. Trust me, I know the signs. Gambling addiction, yes, but not drugs."

"He can't take all of Loraine's money, though," I said. "There has to be some for the house and groceries, cat food for Roger, her doctor's appointments, things like that. If he keeps losing her money, they're going to run out. Then where is he going to get more?"

"Well, here's a thought," Jerry said. "He may not be using drugs, but he might be dealing drugs to pay for his gambling habit."

"How can we find out?" I didn't like the idea of hanging

around Betty's on the off chance Lon would make a deal in the parking lot. "He's probably had enough of you."

"I think Willow would be up for the job. She does a very convincing addict. I can text her and see if she's available."

We pulled over into a church parking lot and Jerry sent his text. In a few minutes Willow replied. She was available and could come to Betty's right away. As much as I disliked the thought of dealing with yet another of Jerry's friends, at least Willow wasn't trying to recruit him for a con, and he wouldn't be directly involved in this plan.

Jerry sent her Lon's description and what we needed to find out. Her reply was a check mark.

"What do we do now?" I asked. "I'm guessing Willow won't need our help."

"Nope. We'll go home and wait for her report. She'll signal if she runs into a problem, but she never has a problem."

***

Well, I had a problem. I wasn't sure how long we'd have to wait or what sort of danger we might have sent Willow into. It would take her at least thirty minutes to drive from Parkland to Celosia. Then she'd have to hang around the parking lot at Betty's until Lon came out. Or maybe she'd go in and scope things out first. I had no idea how she worked a con.

It was past midnight when Jerry's phone chimed. I watched his face as he read Willow's text, but his expression remained calm. "Okay," he said to me when he'd finished and sent her a reply. "Willow says we owe her one hundred and twenty-five bucks, which is just about what I won from Lon, and what would we like her to do with the cocaine?"

"Keep it in a safe place," I said. "It's evidence."

CHAPTER FOURTEEN

That night, my dreams were so scrambled and full of anxiety, I jerked awake several times. I dreamed Jerry was slowly morphing into Big Mike, and although I told him to stop, he kept turning away as if he couldn't or didn't want to hear me. I dreamed Nadia's ghost dressed like Cleopatra rose from a pyramid in the field behind our house. Scariest of all, I dreamed my mother found out Big Mike had bought the wrong kind of sneakers for her wedding gift, left him, and came to live with me. There was a way out of this maze of confusion, but I found myself running around in circles and up against dead ends.

Good grief, I thought. I'm in my own personal crop circle.

And something else kept circling in my mind, something Lon had said to Jerry.

Women can't keep secrets.

What did he mean by that? Was that why his conversation with Nadia at Deely's hadn't been all good memories and how've you been? Had she told a secret that she should have kept?

Because I had such a restless night, I overslept. By the time I got my eyes completely open, Jerry had already left for Deely's. I was always amazed by how quietly he could get up and leave without waking me, but his various cons and schemes had often called for stealth mode. My phone beeped annoyingly until I reached for it, knocking it to the floor. I scrambled for it, hoping it was someone with a clue, any clue, but it was Eloise Michaels from the Woman's Improvement Society and Miss SkinkFest Pageant Committee.

"Hello, Madeline. I hope I'm not calling too early."

It was eight thirty and Thursday already. I had really overslept. "No, no," I said. "What can I do for you?"

"We're having our final planning session at ten thirty this morning at Deely's if you can come. It shouldn't take too long."

I was suddenly awake. There was something I needed to ask her. "I'll be there," I said.

"Thank you! Oh, and we're asking the judges to wear stripes at the pageant, too, if you have something."

"I'll see what I can do." I almost asked if I needed to wear a detachable tail, too, but decided that was way too snarky. It wasn't fair to Eloise that I was still in my morning mood.

***

I managed to get myself together in about thirty minutes. I even stopped by my office to pick up the mail and stopped in at Flair for Fashion where I found a striped blouse that would go well with one of my dark skirts. There was a commotion further down the street where the SkinkFest banner had come undone yet again, and men were up in the cherry picker and on the ladder of the fire truck attempting to fasten it back. This involved a lot of shouting and conflicting opinions about the best way to secure the banner.

My morning mood improved considerably when I entered

Deely's and Jerry greeted me.

"You look like you could use a bacon biscuit," he said.

"Always."

He left to make my breakfast. I sat down at the counter. R.W. Jessup called to me from the Geezer Club corner.

"Madeline, you have any idea who made that mess in my corn field?"

"I'm working on it."

Horace and Frank didn't help the situation by making scary "oooo" noises and singing the theme from *Close Encounters*. R.W. fussed at them until they laughed and promised to stop.

Jerry brought my biscuit and a cup of coffee. "Glad to see you're awake. You were making all sorts of noises in your sleep."

I didn't want him to know part of my dream revealed my continuing anxiety about his future. I stirred my coffee. "Well, I had a fine mash-up of nightmares. I feel so bad for Mr. Conrad, plus worrying over Bill and wondering what Lon's up to. The perfect storm."

Jerry was called back to the kitchen. I ate my biscuit and surveyed the diner. The early morning crowd had come and gone, and now the regulars wandered in to their favorite booths. Conversation swirled around me. SkinkFest was the main topic, but folks were also chatting about the crop circle, Fogarty's crazy ideas, and the usual gossip, church business, and health issues that Celosians discussed. Before moving to Celosia, I'd worked for a large investigations company that relied on a computer network of information. Deely's was my information center, and it hadn't failed me yet.

Eloise arrived a little after ten, wearing her khaki slacks and striped blouse. I joined her in her booth. After she ordered her breakfast, she told me everything was ready for Miss SkinkFest.

"What about publicity?" I asked.

"Oh, the local radio station has been very good about that," Eloise said, "and there's been an article in the paper every day this week. Posters are up in every window in town, and we've taken flyers around to all the hotels and businesses. I made sure of that."

"Sounds like everything is under control," I said. "I wanted to ask you if you knew anything about the Thompson family. I understand their son Patrick had a fatal accident at Carson's Cave seven years ago. Do you recall anything about that?"

"I remember reading about it in the paper," she said.

"Did you know the family?"

"Not very well. I invited Mrs. Thompson to join the Improvement Society, but she declined. A bit stand-offish. But she had her hands full with Patrick. He was always taking risks, skateboarding down the Baptist Church steps, jumping off the Point Richardson Bridge, swinging from trees like Tarzan. It's a shame about his accident, but I have to say it wasn't a surprise."

"Are the Thompsons still in Celosia?"

"No, they moved away after Patrick's accident." She glanced at her watch. "I'm going to pick up the prize ribbons for the pageant and make sure there's a table and chairs for the judges. You're sure you have something striped to wear?"

I showed her my striped blouse, which she approved. When our meeting was over, I returned to my seat at the counter and had an unexpected call from Chief Brenner.

"Well, whatever you said to your ex-husband worked, Madeline. He's dropped the belligerent attitude and is being much more cooperative."

Thank God. "Is he still a person of interest?"

"I'll keep you informed," he said, which was his way of saying, "We are in charge of this investigation."

"There's something I'd like to know," I said. "Does Celosia have a problem with drugs?"

"Every town has a problem with drugs," he said, "even a small town like Celosia. You'd be surprised."

"Has it been a serious problem for some time, or just recently?"

"It's always around in one form or another. Why are you asking? Does this have anything to do with Nadia Conrad's murder?" He didn't add, "If you've found a connection, you'd better tell me," but that was implied.

But I didn't have a connection, only a suspicion. "No, I'm just looking into Nadia's friends."

I thanked him and ended the call. Jerry refilled my coffee cup. "Is Bill off the hook?"

"Not yet," I said.

"You're thinking hard enough for me to hear you way back in the kitchen."

No one was sitting on either side of me, but I kept my voice low to keep anyone curious from overhearing. "It's something Lon said to you. 'Women can't keep secrets.' I wonder if Nadia knew about his drug dealing, and that's the secret she was going to tell."

"Would she rat on an old friend?"

"An old friend who may have been dealing for a long time."

Jerry frowned in thought. "I don't know. If Lon's been dealing for years, let's say even in high school, why would Nadia decide to tell his secret now? What would she gain, except the possibility of being murdered to insure her silence?"

More folks started coming in, and Jerry had to return to the kitchen. I sat for a while trying to make all the pieces of this puzzle fit and decided I needed a quiet place to think.

***

My office was the perfect place, but when I stopped by there was someone waiting by my door.

Rodman Fogarty.

He looked up from his phone. "Oh, there you are, Madeline. I was just sending you a text. I wonder if I might have a moment of your time?"

"Of course," I said. I unlocked the door, and he bowed, motioning me in.

He was impressed by the décor. "What a charming room! Did you paint the walls? I understand you are quite the artist."

"Yes, thanks." I indicated the chair in front of my desk. "What can I do for you?"

He took another turn around the room before settling in the chair. "First and foremost, I want to invite you to come star gaze at Carson's Crater tonight. I'll be giving a lecture on the astounding coincidences between our constellations and alien life forms, plus how one's zodiac sign can influence your life choices. The weather is supposed to be perfect. We'll begin at nine o'clock."

"Thank you," I said. "That sounds interesting."

"No chance of some bucolic bully plowing up the constellations," he said wryly.

"That is a shame about the crop circle."

"It's more than a shame. It's a crime. I've already lodged a complaint with the Crop Circle Association."

"There's a Crop Circle Association?"

"Indeed there is. Those farm boys will be sorry they destroyed one of the wonders of the paranormal world."

I didn't mention that crop circles weren't permanent wonders.

Fogarty had finished venting. "The second reason I'm here is to ask you about Celosia. What brought you and Jerry here, if I may ask? It's a charming little town, but a bit quiet for the two of you, isn't it?"

Oh, you'd be surprised, I thought. "Jerry's Uncle Val left him the Eberlin House, and we decided this would be a good town for me to set up my agency."

"I see. You know, I never imagined Jerry would settle down, but he seems content to fry bacon in a small town diner. It's hard to believe he'd give up such a stellar career."

Well, he's trying to give it up, I thought, but people like you keep coming out of the woodwork. And what's with all the questions? "He enjoys working at Deely's."

Fogarty had another question. "Did you have your wedding in Celosia? I've been quite remiss about congratulating you on your marriage. Lots of Jerry's friends and former partners must have been there, Honor and Rick and Derek, and Willow. Lovely girl, so talented."

"Actually, it was a private ceremony in Parkland," I said.

"Has it been five years already?"

"Two years."

This seemed to square with whatever he was thinking. "Well, I'm sure he was off running cons before you snagged him, my dear. Has he told you about his adventures?"

I've been involved in more than I liked, I wanted to say, but I waited, curious to see where he was going. "A few."

He sat back and tapped one long finger on his lips. "Hmm,

mostly in North Carolina, I would think."

"As far as I know."

"Not, say, Florida? Lots of excitement down there."

"He hasn't mentioned Florida."

"Oh, he was probably traveling everywhere. I know I was."

Pieces of his conversation fell into place. Willow had said that Fogarty spent five years in prison for a con he ran in Florida. She'd also mentioned he was looking for the person who had ratted on him. Did he think Jerry was the one? "You'd have to ask Jerry," I said.

For a moment, there was a spark of pure hatred in his eyes, quickly followed by a smile and a flourish of his hand. "Of course. I don't mean to bore you with all my questions about the past, Madeline. I truly am much more invested in my pursuit of alien knowledge."

He stood and prepared to go. He rearranged his suit jacket and gave me another bow. "Thank you for your time, Madeline. I shall see you at nine tonight. Who knows what the stars will reveal?"

Who knows, indeed? I thought.

***

I had to share this interesting visit with Jerry, so I walked back down the street to Deely's. As I related the high points of Fogarty's conversation, Jerry was amused at first, but when I got to the part about my suspicions that Fogarty thought Jerry had sold him out, his expression darkened.

"So that's the main reason he's here," Jerry said. "But I would never rat on anyone. That's the quickest way to get yourself booted out of the organization—or worse. Besides, his con took place in

Florida. When was I ever in Florida?"

"He tried his best to figure out if I knew anything," I said.

"Well, I'll set him straight, if he'll believe me," he said. "What do you want to do next? Have you talked to all of Nadia's friends?"

"Everyone in her special group," I said. And then I stopped, my coffee cup half way to my mouth. "Wait a minute." I set my cup down. "When I asked Kathy Holly if she'd seen Nadia last week, she said she hadn't seen her or heard from her since Nadia moved to Parkland. She'd been chatting along until I asked that question, and then dropped into the Bitter Zone."

"Nadia visited everyone else, but not her."

"Exactly. And since Kathy's apparently still stuck in High School Jealousy Mode, she took this very personally."

"Personally enough to attack Nadia?"

"Can you be that annoyed for seven years?"

"Sure. I know people who were born annoyed."

My high school years hadn't been a lot of fun, but I'd left them far behind me. "Was she that desperate for acceptance? This is another level of needy."

"Or," Jerry said, "it wasn't just acceptance she was looking for."

This hadn't occurred to me, and I felt really dumb for not seeing it. "She was in love with someone in the group."

"Would you like to bet that someone was Nadia?"

"You know, I haven't talked with Kathy since Nadia was found," I said. "Lon mentioned that she pushed herself into their group. Coreen said something similar, that Kathy was not welcome, but she always managed to tag along anyway. What if she took the photo of the four friends at the cave?"

"That would mean she was there when Patrick had his accident."

"I'm calling her right now."

There was no answer, and no message that the mailbox was full. Hmm, that seemed odd. Even if she was out of town, I was pretty sure she'd answer her phone. Kathy had impressed me as one of those talkers who never stop for a breath, but just sail on to the next topic.

"You want to stop by her house?" Jerry asked. He glanced at the clock. "If you can wait a few minutes, I'll go with you."

"That might be a good idea," I said.

CHAPTER FIFTEEN

Kathy Holly lived in Forest Grove, which was another up-scale neighborhood. It was not as fancy as Silver Lakes, but it was definitely a classy development. Kathy's house was a two story brick mansion with white columns surrounded by neatly trimmed bushes. Jerry parked the Jeep in the driveway, and we walked up a flagstone pathway to the etched glass door sporting a wreath of realistic-looking sunflowers.

I rang the doorbell. We waited. And waited.

The garage door was up with a mid-sized white sedan parked inside. I rang the doorbell again and used the front door knocker. Still no answer.

Jerry had brought along his special keys. The door was locked and there was a deadbolt lock, as well. "This one would take too long to pick," he said. "Let's go round to the back."

The back of the house featured a brick patio with the kind of white wrought iron furniture that always looks uncomfortable. Tall lines of bushes and cedar trees made barriers between Kathy's house and the houses on either side. Jerry had no trouble with the back door, which led into a large kitchen, gleaming with stainless steel appliances.

"Kathy?" I called. "Hello, anybody home?"

We moved quietly through the house and stopped still when we reached the living room. Up to now, the house had been tidy to the point of sterile, but the living room walls were filled with framed photographs, all sizes, all amazing. Hummingbirds caught with the sun shimmering on their ruby throats. Sunflowers brilliantly yellow against a blue sky. Cascades of red and gold autumn leaves tumbling to a brook. Silhouettes of trees against a twilight sky. The whole room was a kaleidoscope of images and colors.

And there among all the nature photos was a framed copy of the picture I'd seen in Coreen's bedroom, all four smiling friends with Carson's Cave behind them.

Jerry quietly ventured down the hallway to look into a few more rooms. He motioned me to a room on the right. Kathy's office had a computer, but instead of books and filing cabinets, several tripods leaned against the wall, and the shelves were filled with boxes of camera lenses, filters, and expensive-looking cameras and cases.

The other rooms on this floor were a guest room and a den. Both rooms were nicely if dully furnished and bereft of photographs. We went back down the hall to the entry way. As we climbed the stairs, I called Kathy's name again. Maybe she was taking a shower or a nap. If she was, we were going to scare the hell out of her.

"I don't think she's home, Mac," Jerry said. "The place is too still."

"I hope to God we aren't going to find another dead body," I said.

At the top of the stairs, Jerry held out a hand to stop me. "Maybe not a dead body, but something's not right. Look."

There were bits of paper scattered on the light blue carpet.

"I don't think Kathy would have left a mess in her perfect home," he said.

We moved cautiously to the master bedroom where we came upon the scene of what appeared to be a frantic search. Drawers had been yanked open. The closet was a jumble of clothes dangling from hangers and piled on the floor. Plastic containers had been pulled from under the bed, their contents spilled. Ripped paper was everywhere.

"It's a bit late for spring cleaning," Jerry said. "Wonder what they were looking for?"

"And who was looking for it," I said.

"We'd better check the other rooms."

The other bedroom and the sitting room were as pristine as the rest of the house. Relieved we hadn't found Kathy injured or dead, we returned to the master bedroom. Someone felt the need to tear up the papers, so I needed to know what was on them. But this room was a potential crime scene, so gathering up a pile to take home was out. Fortunately, the intruder was a ripper not a shredder, and some of the pieces were large enough to read.

"Jerry, see if you can get pictures of what's written on the papers. We might be able to piece them together." I soon found a pattern in the scraps I photographed. "These look like handwritten receipts."

"These do, too," he said.

I quickly scrolled through my photos to the picture of the Evil Note. The handwriting was a match. "Kathy's our note writer," I said,

"Here's one made out to 'Prin.' The rest is missing. Principle, perhaps?"

I found another piece with enough writing to read. "I've got 'onrad' here. Conrad, maybe? But what's this 'ancy'? Was someone trying to spell Nancy instead of Nadia? And here's an 'ud.'"

He walked around the edge of the room, being careful not to step on any of the papers. He stopped and gestured towards a thicker piece of colored paper. "This might explain it."

The paper was a corner torn from a picture showing a glowing red pulse of light.

"Recognize this alien?" Jerry said.

"It's a piece of a movie poster," I said. "A poster for *Encounter With Doom.*"

Now I understood. "Not Nancy. Fancy. Nadia's nickname from the movie. And the Prin must be Princess, Coreen's nickname, and the 'ud' is Dud, Lon's nickname. Kathy's been writing receipts to Nadia, Coreen, and Lon."

And the receipts were for hefty fees of some kind. No information on the entry line, just a happy face. One receipt to Princess was for two thousand dollars. Receipts to Fancy and Dud were smaller, but still chunks of money. The bulk of the torn papers were these puzzling receipts.

Why were they paying money to Kathy? What was the money for?

Unless…

Solving murders and dealing with Jerry's friends had given me a much more cynical awareness. I seriously doubted Kathy was taking up money for a memorial fund. She'd been trying her best to get into the special group. Perhaps she tagged along to Carson's Cave, saw what really happened to Patrick, and had been blackmailing the remaining members of the clique.

"The note you found said, 'all secrets kept, all debts paid,'"

Jerry said. "The group has been paying her for keeping a secret, and there's only one thing they all have in common."

"Patrick's accident," I said. "They were all at the cave when it happened. Is it possible one of them is responsible for Patrick's death, and they lied to the police? They were teenagers. They must have been scared."

"Well, the secret was kept, but apparently, they're still paying off the debt."

"I'll bet that's it," I said. "They made a pact and promised each other not to tell what really happened. But later on, Kathy decided she finally had power over these people who never really accepted her and started charging them for her silence. Using their nicknames is a snarky way of saying, 'Gotcha.'" I looked around the room. "But I don't think she'd trash her own bedroom. Someone came looking for those receipts, and only three people would have known about them. We know it's not Nadia."

"Lon's got my vote."

"But Coreen's been very evasive. She knows more than she's telling."

We went back down the stairs and out the back door. Jerry locked the door and used the tail of his shirt to wipe the doorknob. "If I were still in Con World, I'd be worried about Kathy," he said.

"Do I call Chief Brenner and report a possible break in at Kathy's house?" I asked. "He'll want to know how I know."

"You can tell him you noticed the back door was open. That's actually true."

"And I just decided to wander upstairs?"

"You thought you heard a cry for help."

I had to laugh. "Jerry, honest to God."

"How many times have I told you? Always have a story ready."

We got into my car and I called Chief Brenner. He listened to me and then said, "And you were there because?"

"She hasn't answered any of my phone calls and messages, which I find odd, because I messaged I wanted to ask her about Nadia, and she loves to talk about her high school days. When I went to her house and knocked on the door, there was no answer," I said.

"Any signs of a break in?"

I didn't look at Jerry. "I noticed the back door was open. I was concerned, so I went inside. Someone had trashed her bedroom." I didn't mention that the bedroom was upstairs. "I promise you I did not disturb a thing."

"All right," the Chief said, but he didn't sound happy. "I'll send someone out to have a look."

He ended the call, and I blew out the breath I hadn't realized I was holding.

"See?" Jerry said. "That wasn't so hard, was it?"

CHAPTER SIXTEEN

At home, Jerry fixed cheese sandwiches and tomato soup for our late lunch. I continued to call Kathy's number with no success.

"Okay," I said. "Time to call Coreen."

"She might shut you down again."

"Well, she can try, but there's something else I could bring up."

When I called Coreen, I could tell by her tone she was still not interested in talking to me.

"This is not a good time, Madeline. My husband and I are heading off to our beach house, and we're in the midst of packing."

"I understand," I said, "but recently I came across a very interesting movie called *Encounter With Doom*, which I believe was your high school group's favorite. I just have a couple of questions about it."

There was a long pause, and then she said, "I suppose I could spare you a few minutes."

"Sure," I said. "I'll be right there." I ended the call and turned to Jerry. "She and her husband are leaving town."

"That suggests a couple of things," he said.

"Yes. Such as, she's the murderer and making her getaway, or she's afraid she's next."

"If she's leaving town today, her house will be empty tomorrow," Jerry said hopefully.

As much as I liked this idea, I had to say, "Let me talk to her first."

***

Coreen met me at her front door, phone to her ear. She looked impeccably stylish, as usual, in white shorts and a pink and white halter top.

"Come in," she said. "Yes, I'm still here," she said into the phone. "That's right. And make sure you water the lilies at the back. Yes, check on them every day. I don't know exactly how long we'll stay. I'll call you if my plans change." She ended the call. "Excuse the mess, Madeline. I never know how much to pack."

The mess was a stack of pink luggage by the stairway. "Must be nice to get away for a while," I said.

"Oh, yes, and no doubt the beach house will need something done. It always does. Now what's all this about *Encounter With Doom?* That's ancient history."

I turned my phone so she could see the piece of the receipt with "Prin" on it. "I wonder if you know anything about this."

She looked at the picture for a long time before answering. "No."

"Here's what I think," I said. "I think this receipt was made out to Princess, your high school nickname." I showed her another picture. "And this says Princess paid four thousand dollars to Kathy Holly. And here's another piece with Fancy's name. That would be

Nadia. There's one for Dud, Lon's nickname. Princess and Fancy and Dud are all characters in *Encounter With Doom*."

Coreen was a pale woman, but she managed to go a shade lighter. "That doesn't mean anything."

"Kathy went along with you and Nadia and Lon to Carson's Cave September 17 seven years ago, didn't she? She took that photograph of the four of you. There's a copy hanging up in her house."

"What if she did? What are you getting at?"

"That was the day of Patrick's accident. Here's what I think happened. One or maybe all of you caused Patrick's death, and you made a pledge to cover it up. After a few years, when you all starting doing well and had a little money, Kathy saw her opportunity. She knew you'd all lied to the police. She's been blackmailing you for at least the last year, hasn't she?"

Coreen's voice was low and tense. "You cannot tell anyone about this."

"What really happened that day at Carson's Cave?" I asked.

"I didn't kill Patrick!"

"Then explain things to me."

She crossed her arms and gave me a cold appraising stare as if trying to decide what to tell me. "I'll admit I was angry with him," she said. "I'd found out he'd cheated on me with Nadia. But Nadia was angry, too, because he'd lied to her, and Lon was angry because of the way Patrick treated Nadia. We were one big furious collection of teen angst. We were screaming at each other, and when Patrick fell, we—we just stood there. Maybe one of us pushed him. I don't know. Whatever happened, we all buried it and did our best to forget about it." She paused and rubbed her forehead. "Then last year, we started getting these—these bills from Kathy. 'Pay up, or I'll tell.' God, it's been awful."

"Why didn't you tell the police the truth?"

"Are you insane? And have one or all of us arrested for murder? Nadia would have broken her grandfather's heart. Lon's mother would have been devastated. We decided to let it be. Hoping that Kathy would stop at some point. Or—"

"Or what?"

"Or we'd think of something. But we never did."

"Someone broke into her house and tore up all these receipts, and she's not answering her phone. Do you know where she is?"

She leaned forward and emphasized every word. "No. And. I. Don't. Care. I would be glad to have her out of my life, the conniving little bitch, but there's no way I would set foot in her house."

"Where were you this morning?" I asked.

"In Rossboro, speaking at their garden club. And before you accuse me of anything else, I didn't kill Nadia, either. I'm the victim here!"

"Have you seen Lon recently?" I asked.

She stopped cold, and for a long moment I thought she wasn't going to answer. When she did, her voice was tightly controlled. "He wouldn't do anything to Nadia."

"Not even if she had decided she couldn't live with the secret anymore?"

"That's absurd. She lived with it for seven years. Why tell the police now?"

"Nadia was killed in the cave last Saturday," I said. "That was September 17, the anniversary of Patrick's accident. I think Lon suggested—or maybe it was her idea—that they go to the cave to remember Patrick. Lon tried to convince her not to go to the police, and when she said no, he was afraid the police would find out he was dealing drugs."

She gave a short laugh. "What are you talking about? Lon always liked to gamble, but dealing drugs? That's absurd."

Was Coreen keeping yet another secret? Had Lon managed to keep this from the others? Or was she lying to protect him? "There's proof."

"Then go bother Lon. I don't want any part of this."

"Coreen, all this will come out now," I said. "You know that."

She gave me a contemptuous look. "All this would have stayed buried if you hadn't come along. You need to leave."

***

I'd just gotten into my car and hooked my seat belt when Chief Brenner called with the news that his officers had found evidence of foul play at Kathy Holly's house.

"I'd like to see you in my office," he said. "Now."

***

Chief Brenner leaned both arms on his desk. "Full story," he said. "What were you doing at Kathy Holly's house and what did you see?"

I had pushed my luck far enough. "I really did need to speak with her, and I did not tamper with any evidence," I said. "Is Kathy all right?"

"We found evidence of a struggle in her garage," he said. "Her car door was unlocked and her pocketbook was on the front seat. There were scuff marks on the garage floor and gardening tools and flower pots had been knocked off the shelves. One of her shoes was found under the car. It appears she was trying to escape an intruder and was carried off."

I swallowed hard. Jerry and I had not gone into the garage. We might have been able to prevent this. Or not.

The chief had also thought of this. He sat back. "If this intruder had still been there, he might've killed you and Jerry, ever think of that?" He gave me a long serious look. "Madeline, you know I've been fairly lenient with you poking around. I can't deny your investigations have gotten results. But you are going to leave this one alone. He let that sink in. "I don't want to arrest you for withholding information or obstructing this investigation, but I will if I think jail would be a safer place for you right now. Do not, I repeat, do not go into anyone's house unless you have been invited. Got that?"

"Yes," I said.

"That goes for Jerry, too."

"The neighbors didn't see or hear anything?"

"Unfortunately, Ms. Holly's house is surrounded by trees and bushes."

I was going to take the "withholding information" warning seriously. "Chief, you might want to question Coreen Overmeyer and Lon Forest."

"Mrs. Overmeyer's husband vouched for her. And we've already talked with Mr. Forest. He said he'd been with his mother all day, and she affirmed this. Anything else?

I shook my head.

"Then go home."

***

I ran and hopped into my car and called Jerry. "Kathy's missing and Lon told the police he'd been with his mother all day. We'd better check out Carson's Cave."

CHAPTER SEVENTEEN

When we arrived at the crater, we spotted the beige Oldsmobile parked near the entrance to Carson's Cave. I parked my car close by. There was no sign of Lon.

We turned on our phones' flashlights and cautiously entered the cave.

"Watch your head," Jerry said, indicating a cracked beam above.

"That doesn't look very secure," I said.

We had to stoop to get in, but then the cave widened enough that we could stand. We walked further in until we came upon a dead end of solid rock where we found Kathy sprawled on the ground. I quickly checked and found a pulse. Then a shadow fell across her body. Jerry and I looked up to see Lon Forest holding a shotgun and blocking the cave entrance.

"Oh, hello," Lon said, his voice eerily calm.

We stood and faced him. His expression was difficult to see, but then he recognized Jerry, and his voice became harsh. "You! You stole my money. What the hell are you doing here?" Then he glared at me. "Oh, I see. She sent you into Betty's. You're in this together to cheat me."

"We can discuss this later," I said, "But we need to get Kathy to the hospital."

"No," he said. "It's her own fault if she's hurt. She was awfully foolish to go into this cave alone."

I didn't like the way his voice changed back to calm. "What are you doing here, Lon? Why kidnap Kathy and bring her here? Unless she knew something you wanted kept secret."

He flinched at the word "secret."

I'd hoped to keep him occupied so Jerry could move into a position to disarm him, but the cave entrance was too narrow. Jerry took a careful step to one side, but Lon saw him move and swung the shotgun around to point it at his chest.

Jerry put both hands up and backed away. "You may have a quarrel with me, but Mac hasn't done anything to you."

"Oh, really?" he said and gave me a sneer. "Mom said you'd come by and snooped in my bedroom. This ought to be the end of your snooping." He glared at Jerry. "And taking care of you is an unexpected bonus."

"So you're going to get rid of everybody?" I said. "That doesn't make a lot of sense. No, wait, I guess it does. You have to get rid of anyone who might know about Kathy Holly's blackmail scheme. But that's not the only secret, is it? Everyone in your group knew what happened to Patrick, and it wasn't an accident. Everyone decided to lie to the police, even when Kathy began the blackmail. But Nadia got to the point where she couldn't live with the secret anymore. I think she was going to tell the police the truth, and then they'd find out not only did everyone in your group lie to them about Patrick, but you've been dealing drugs."

For a moment, his hand holding the shotgun trembled. "We all swore to keep it a secret, and then that damned Kathy who was never one of us started her threats. Nadia thought if she left town Kathy would leave her alone. But she didn't." His voice trailed off.

"Nadia wanted to be here on September 17," I said. "The anniversary of Patrick's death. Patrick's family had moved away and there was no gravestone or memorial, just the cave. She wanted to go to the cave one last time and then no more lies. And you came with her, maybe to try to convince her not to tell the secret."

His voice was barely audible. "I begged her not to tell."

"How angry were you, Lon?"

He took a step back. "Just a couple of shots, and the whole ceiling will fall in. Nobody'll find Kathy. Nobody'll find you, either. Give me your phones."

I started to hand him my phone and purposely dropped it. Lon kept his eyes on me as he bent to retrieve it, giving Jerry the chance to throw his phone as hard as he could at Lon's head, hitting the man in the forehead. When Lon staggered back, Jerry jumped forward and grabbed Lon's wrist, forcing him back, the gun pointed up. Lon was larger and heavier than Jerry, so I joined the fight. The three of us grappled and struggled until Lon fired the gun. The blast hit the cracked beam holding up the ceiling, and the cave wall collapsed.

Jerry caught me around the waist and pulled me back as the wall fell on top of Lon, burying him under rocks and timbers. When the terrifying noise ceased, I realized that the debris closed off the cave, leaving me, Jerry, and Kathy trapped inside in complete darkness. Jerry and I took several minutes to catch our breath. Then we felt around for my phone. It was buried with Lon, along with Jerry's.

"Okay," I said with far more confidence than I felt. "We can figure this out."

After a fruitless search in the dark, we pushed against the wall of debris that blocked our way out. It was solid. So we started digging, moving aside as many rocks and as much dirt as we could until we needed a break. Jerry and I sat together, leaning against the cave wall.

"Who knows we came here?" he asked.

"No one."

"Who knows Kathy came here?"

"Besides us? Lon."

"What are the chances he survived the cave in?"

"Not too good," I said. "And even if he did, he wouldn't tell anyone where we were."

"If I had some light, I could explore further into the cave and see if there is another entrance."

"And possibly cause more of it to collapse." I leaned closer to him. "Someone's bound to see the cars parked outside. We'll just have to wait for morning and hope the rest of the cave doesn't collapse."

"Maybe part of Lon is sticking out," Jerry said. "That would be a good clue."

I had to chuckle. "You know, I really didn't want this case to have such a direct parallel to *Aida*."

"We'll rest a while longer and keep digging," he said. "No tragic opera ending for us."

***

It was hard work in total darkness, but we continued our efforts. We managed to create a tiny peephole, big enough for us to realize the only light was a faint gleam of moonlight, and there was a good chance we would not be found until morning, if then. Even as small as it was, the pinpoint of light encouraged us to work faster, halting when we realized we'd reached a sagging timber.

"I'm afraid if we keep digging we'll bring down even more of the roof," Jerry said. "Feel along here." His hand guided mine to the edge of the beam. "Feel how it's cracked? Feel these big rocks weighing down on it? We'd better stop."

"How about if we work on the other side?"

"We could try. Carefully."

We felt our way to the opposite side of the debris. Cautiously, we pulled rocks free and put them aside. We worked until we heard an ominous creaking sound.

"Uh, oh," Jerry said. "Time to move away."

"I think I hear something."

"Aliens, no doubt, pissed that we messed up their cave."

I scrambled to my feet. "No, I heard a car." I hurried to the little bit of light. "Hey! Is someone out there? We need help!"

Jerry added his voice. We shouted as loudly as we could and were finally rewarded by a muffled voice.

"Madeline? Jerry? Is that you?"

"Yes!" we shouted.

"Good heavens!" the voice said. "Are you all right? I'm calling for help."

I couldn't see Jerry's face, but his voice was filled with surprise. "That's Fogarty."

I had forgotten that Fogarty was leading another group of believers to star gaze over the crater tonight.

Rodman Fogarty's voice was also surprised. "What are you doing in there?"

"Call nine-one-one and I'll tell you all about it when we get out," Jerry said.

In about fifteen minutes, the police arrived with a rescue team. It took them another hour and a half to clear away the debris and shore up the cave so that Jerry and I could get out and Kathy could be safely carried to an ambulance. Lon Forest's body was carried off by the medical examiner's team. Jerry and I declined medical aid. Aside from scratches and my broken fingernails, we were fine and delighted to be out in the evening air.

Chief Brenner was not delighted to find us in the middle of yet another crime scene. It took a while for me to explain about the high school clique and Kathy Holly's blackmail scheme.

"So that's what all those torn receipts were about," he said. "And you think Lon Forest was responsible for Patrick Thompson's death?"

"No one knew for certain, and the three friends had kept it secret for years," I said. "Now that Lon's dead, we may never know the truth. But all evidence points to Lon as Nadia's killer, and he would want to silence Kathy, as well. But there's something else Lon wanted to keep secret."

Up went his eyebrows. "Oh?"

"He was dealing drugs. I don't know if Nadia knew that, but if she came to you to confess the group lied about Patrick's death, your investigation may have led to Lon and his deals, and he couldn't have that come out."

Chief Brenner eyed me for a long moment and then said, "I suppose you have proof of this?"

Jerry gave me a glance and spoke up before I could answer. "Mac had her suspicions, so I convinced him I was looking for a quick fix."

"He believed you?"

"I'm pretty good at making people believe me," Jerry said with a grin.

He didn't add, "Even you, Chief," but I realized what he was doing. He was keeping Willow completely out of the picture.

"I met him in the parking lot at Betty's Bingo Bar," he continued. "You know it?"

"I am very familiar with Betty's Bingo Bar," the chief said.

"He was happy to sell me a gram of cocaine. I can bring it to you tomorrow."

"I think you'd better." He transferred his dark gaze to me. "Are you okay?"

"Yes, thanks."

"Next time, you might want to consider calling the police before you two decide to confront a suspected killer in a cave. Only there'd better not be a next time."

He returned to his investigation.

"Next time, I'll be a lot more careful," I said to Jerry. "Is Professor Fogarty still here? We need to thank him."

Fogarty was leaning against his car, his arms folded. He accepted Jerry's thanks and then scowled. "Well, I missed a golden opportunity to get rid of you."

Jerry wasn't fazed by this remark. "That's really why you came to Celosia, isn't it?"

Fogarty didn't deny it. "I always resented you, you little upstart, coming in and ruining a perfectly good set up. I just knew I was the one in line to take over the organization. I had to be! I was the one who put in all those long hard years, traveling around dinky God forsaken towns, dealing with the yokels, and putting on tacky displays to get them to part with their grubby cash. Then finally

Big Mike lets me in on the really good cons. Finally! And what happens? Somebody blows my cover and I spend five years in jail. Well, now I know who that somebody was."

"You've got the wrong guy," Jerry said. "You were long gone by the time Big Mike recruited me."

"Yes, but I kept in touch with Willow and the others at the pawn shop. Of course, they wouldn't tell me where you were, in case you had a con going, but everyone seemed to think you were Big Mike's likely choice. I looked all over for you, and then I had a stroke of luck. I happened to be channel surfing in my hotel in Parkland and a show came on called *From Crown to Crime*, and there you were, chatting away with your lovely wife about how damn clever she is at solving murders in your charming little town. From there it was easy to book myself at the Celosia Little Theater and inquire about you at the local diner. You're quite the big noise, aren't you? Both of you."

Jerry remained calm. "So what do you want? You want back in the clubhouse? That's not my call. Besides, I turned him down."

Fogarty continued his rant. "To think that he'd choose someone like you instead of —what?"

"I turned him down. I said no, thanks."

Fogarty's eyes bulged. "Nobody turns Big Mike down! Are you insane? Do you have a death wish? When Big Mike wants something, he gets it."

"If you'd shut up for a minute, you might learn something."

Fogarty closed his mouth tight.

"Okay," Jerry said, "here's how it is. Big Mike did ask me if I was interested in learning more about his organization. He asked if I'd like to take over some of the duties like recruiting others, helping run some of the more elaborate long cons, overseeing some of the European companies. I told him, as I am now telling you, that I was happy with the way things were. I also promised Mac I would get out of the game. That hasn't been easy, especially when clowns like you keep popping up, but I'm working on it."

"You really want to quit?"

"Before my luck runs out, or someone blows my cover."

Fogarty was silent a few moments, thinking this over. "So it wasn't you?"

"Have you seen your old buddy Sawbuck Sam lately?" Jerry asked.

"What are you implying? That he'd rat me out? That's impossible. We did roof and drive fixing in Tampa. We ran all sorts of cons in some carnivals in Omaha, and then we had a run in Vegas you would not believe. Then we moved on to Reno. We—" He stopped abruptly. "Reno. The games there never came together the way I thought they should. Sam laughed it off. He said, 'Oh, we'll recoup on the next one.' But there was never a next one. Right after that, the cops came knocking on my door."

Jerry let him work it out.

"I never saw Sam after that. Never saw a nickel of that money! I thought the con had failed." His expression hardened. "It was Sam all along. My own partner!"

"Another reason to get out," Jerry said. "There's no one you can really trust."

Fogarty stuck out his hand. "I'm sorry, Jerry. I wronged you, and I apologize."

Jerry shook his hand. "No need. You rescued us. I say we're even."

"For now," Fogarty said, and they both laughed.

CHAPTER EIGHTEEN

Friday morning I visited Loraine to offer my sympathies on the death of her son. She was sitting on her porch, Roger in her lap. As I suspected, she had no idea of Lon's obsession with Nadia or his drug deals and was confused by what had happened to him.

"I know he wrote letters to her and emailed quite often. He was sad when she didn't reply as often as he'd like." She hugged Roger closer. He gave a little growl as if to say, "Okay, that's enough." "I can't understand what went wrong."

"Well, I'm so sorry, Loraine," I said. "Do you have someone staying with you?"

"I've got a cousin over in Raleigh who's coming by today. She's going to see about getting me some in-home care." She gave Roger another hug, which he stoically endured. "Roger and I will get along the best we can."

We sat for a while in companionable silence and then a phone rang from inside the house. As Loraine made an effort to stand, I offered to answer the phone for her.

"Thank you," she said. "It's in the kitchen."

Loraine had a landline, a phone hanging on the wall in her kitchen.

"Loraine Forest's residence," I said. "This is Madeline Maclin."

"Oh, Madeline," the caller said. "This is Juniper. I wanted to tell Loraine I'm really sorry to hear about Lon, and if there's anything I can do for her, for her to let me know. I know I haven't been a good neighbor and overly concerned about myself, but to lose your son and know he killed Nadia and tried to kill you and Kathy—I can't imagine what she's going through."

"I'll be glad to tell her," I said. "How are you doing?"

"Did you ever find my necklace?"

"No," I said, realizing I hadn't even thought of her necklace until just now. "I'll get right back to the search."

"I hope this whole thing at the cave showed you its evil power."

Two can play the Alien Necklace Game. "Yes, but what about the good power of the necklace bringing me and Jerry to Kathy's rescue? And bringing Professor Fogarty and his star gazing group to the crater so he could see my car?"

Silence. "Well," she finally said. "I suppose that's true. But I'd still like you to find it. If I keep it with me, perhaps that will keep its powers calm."

"All right," I said. "Take care. I'll give Loraine your message."

She thanked me and ended the call. I replaced the receiver and returned to the porch. I told Loraine what Juniper had said.

"That's very nice of her," Loraine said. Roger yowled, and she smiled. "See? Roger agrees with me."

Roger jumped off her lap and came over to give me a fresh coat of cat hair. As he wound about my legs, I caught a glimpse of silver and took a closer look at what he wore around his neck. "Loraine, when did you get Roger this collar?"

"Oh, he found it," she said. "Brought it in the other day. He's always finding things in the grass. I thought it would be perfect for him."

Roger gazed up at me, his eyes as green as the stones in his new silver collar. He looked as satisfied as a cat could be. I'd have to tell Loraine that this particular accessory belonged to Juniper. Hopefully, the two women would have a good laugh over it. I was holding in a good laugh right now: Ace detective overlooks obvious alien necklace.

"You're right," I said as much to Roger as to Loraine. "It's perfect."

***

Next I stopped by the police station. Jerry had made a quick trip to Parkland early that morning and retrieved the cocaine Willow had bought from Lon.

The Chief confirmed he'd received the package and that his officers' visit to Betty's Bingo Bar had resulted in several arrests and useful information regarding Lon Forest and his activities.

"What about Kathy and her blackmail scheme?" I asked. "Is she charged with anything?"

"According to North Carolina law, blackmail is a Class 1 misdemeanor. That means if convicted, she could face up to one hundred and twenty days in prison. We've advised her to get a lawyer, but it will be an uphill battle for her. We have all the receipts, as well as a statement from Mrs. Coreen Overmeyer detailing the constant demands for money." He rubbed his forehead, frowning as if he couldn't understand why Coreen and the others had continued to give in to Kathy's demands. "I wish Nadia or Mrs. Overmeyer or even Lon Forest had come forward with this information sooner."

"But then you might have discovered what really happened to Patrick Thompson," I said.

"Who really killed him, you mean? Well, here's the saddest part of this whole story. His death might have actually been an accident, after all."

***

I thought of this as I got into my car to drive home. Four scared and angry teenagers might have thought one of them caused the cave in. Now there was only Coreen, the lone survivor of the group, and I was certain all she cared about was making sure Kathy went to jail.

When my phone rang, it was Bill.

His voice was bright and happy. "Great job, Madeline. I knew I could count on you."

Yes, bright and happy Bill. Never mind that two people were dead. "Thanks."

"I had a long talk with Tina, and we're going to work things out."

Good luck with that. "I hope you can."

There was an awkward pause. He'd thanked me, and to Bill, everything was settled. I didn't have anything else to say to him. It was way too late for him to change his ways. Finally, he said, "Well, good-bye."

I ended the call. I thought I would feel something, but I didn't.

***

I drove home and settled in on the porch. My next phone call was much nicer. Mr. Conrad called to thank me.

"I wanted justice for my girl, and I got it," he said. "Won't bring her back, but least I won't be always wondering what happened to her. That boy, Lon. Stealing his ma's money to gamble with. Always seemed so nice. Shows you how wrong you can be about people, don't it? They got secrets you never would guess."

"You are very right about that," I said.

He thanked me again and ended the call. I sat for a while looking out at the front yard and the oak trees and the wild flowers in the meadow beyond. This seemingly calm little town continued to amaze me by the currents of emotions flowing through, the long-held feuds and disagreements, the obsessions and power plays and downright craziness. Celosia had it all.

Jerry came home from Deely's to report Fogarty was in rare form this morning.

"You should have heard him recounting how he saved us and Kathy from the cave. I smell another book."

"I smell bacon," I said, eying the bag he carried.

He tossed it to me and I caught it. "Two of the best."

I reached into the bag and took out the first one. "All this started with Bill and a couple of biscuits."

Jerry sat down in another rocking chair. "Yes, I recall coming in and being delighted to see him."

"Well, he's gone on his merry way, and I sincerely hope I don't have to deal with him again."

He gave me a sideways glance. "I could make that happen."

"No more cons, remember?" I said.

"Yes, ma'am."

I took a bite of biscuit. "So Fogarty's okay, but has a new King of Con World been crowned?"

Jerry gave the matter a moment of serious thought. "Let me see those wedding photos again."

I handed him my phone. Jerry looked at pictures for a long time and then chuckled.

"What?" I said.

He returned my phone. "Take a look and tell me what you see."

He indicated the picture of Mom and Big Mike in their wedding finery standing in a beautiful garden. "Okay, it's a wonderful picture of both of them looking their absolute best."

"He's sent me a signal. Check out the background."

I took another look. "They're standing beside a tree."

"What kind of tree?"

I looked closer. "A willow." Then I had to chuckle. "A new Queen has been crowned."

"It's an excellent choice. She'll be great."

"And you won't be called upon? You owe her a favor."

"Nope. Keeping her off Chief Brenner's radar was a favor repaid."

"But we always think you're done, and then something else pops up, like Fogarty, for instance."

He paused just long enough for me to know this was a possibility. "I don't want to lie and say no. But Willow knows how I feel, and she's very independent. I think she'll have plenty of other people to choose from."

I was going to have to believe this.

***

After all the excitement, it was fun to relax at SkinkFest that afternoon, although someone sabotaged the skink race by letting all the skinks out. Nothing was left but a bunch of tails wiggling and flopping in the grass. Denisha found this gross, but Austin and most of the other kids laughed as they tried to catch the tails.

To my relief, Miss SkinkFest, Miss Teen SkinkFest, and Little Miss SkinkFest were crowned without controversy. Everyone joined in the spirit of the pageant. Even boys and young men vied for the title of Mr. SkinkFest and Mr. SkinkFest, Junior. I'd never seen so many striped dresses, pants, ties, ribbons, and jackets. Some of the contestants wore striped shoes and socks as well as hats and gloves. One young lady carried a striped umbrella. Another carried a striped fan. Several dogs and cats dressed as lizards accompanied their contestants.

As Jerry and I strolled along Main Street late in the afternoon, the SkinkFest banner flapped in the breeze above us. I recalled seeing the men up on the cherry picker as they restrung it. Then I remembered Jerry telling R.W.'s boys, "I'll take care of it." At the time I thought he was saying their biscuits and fries were on the house, or that he'd see that Fogarty stayed out of their way.

Or maybe he was saying he'd help them find a way to get back at Fogarty and annoy their father.

I recalled how Jerry could be an absolute ninja when he wanted to be. It was entirely possible he slipped out of the house Tuesday night. And it would not surprise me in the least if he could drive and operate a cherry picker. That would be ideal for supervising the creation of a crop circle and for lifting the boys in and out of the field without leaving any tracks. If Jerry was familiar with past crop circle hoaxes—and why wouldn't he be?—he could show R.W.'s sons how to use boards to walk around and make patterns in the field.

Jerry had an absurdly large drink in a green plastic cup labeled "Lucky Lizard Juice." He took a long slurp with the straw. "Another successful case solved for Madeline Maclin Investigations. Excuse me, two cases. You found Juniper's necklace."

"Quite by accident," I said. "However, there's one other thing." At his look of inquiry, I added, "The crop circle."

"Aliens, Mac. Aliens."

"Or a very clever person who likes to play pranks."

He took another slurp. "We may never know."

"Jerry."

He smiled and leaned forward to give me a Lucky Lizard Juice-flavored kiss. "It's a secret."

End